M.R. DOLLSCHNIEDER

Christmas Caper

A Holly Holcraft Cozy Mystery

Contents

Other books by M.R. Dollschnieder

Bones in the Backyard
Fear at the Fall Festival
Body at the Beach

Disaster

I surveyed the devastation with dismay. It looked like a bomb had gone off but the truth was worse. White dust coated every surface and I knew it would take professionals hours to clean up. Unfortunately, there was only me. Apparently mixing all the dry ingredients in a blender was not the shortcut that I thought it would be. With a deep sigh, I looked up.

"I think you were supposed to put the lid on," said my granddaughter Chloe with a grimace on her cute little face. Blue eyes wide under her curly mop. She was standing on a stool at the black granite counter wearing a frilly yellow apron that was too big for her. It had been my grandmother's and always made me happy when I wore it. Seeing it on her recalled my memories of when I was young and cooking with my grandma.

The deep sigh was for the hours of cleaning that I was going to have to do now. Already, Ginger, my Doberman-Shepherd, had begun making giant paw tracks all through the kitchen and out into the living room.

I went to retrieve the vacuum from the hall closet before she could track any more flour through the house and made her sit on the couch while I cleaned the floor. Chloe, who's four, began wiping off the cupboards with a damp towel. The little black kitten who had shown up unexpectedly after my beach trip, meowed up at me with a speck of flour on her little nose. I still hadn't picked out a name for her. "Maybe

Dusty?" I said aloud. Chloe looked at me and shook her head. "You're right, it doesn't fit. We'll just have to keep trying." After the loss of my husband and my cat ten years ago, the idea of replacing the cat was just too painful and then, surprise, this one just showed up unexpectedly in my bed of all places. The universal cat distribution system at its finest I guess.

Twenty minutes later, we got back to our Christmas cookie making, leaving the rest of the mess for later. We would probably spill more stuff on the counters anyway. The cookies were for the Tour of Holiday Homes committee meeting that was going to be held later today at my home and were my favorite, Magic Cookie Bars, filled with coconut, butter, graham cracker crumbs and butterscotch and chocolate chips. The secret ingredient was the sweetened condensed milk that melted it all together.

Homeowners volunteer their houses for the tour and a group of volunteers help decorate the houses. All of the decorations are to be supplied by the homeowners. Traditionally, these are the more expensive homes but I decided to open it up to anyone who wanted to participate this year hoping that we will have a larger area to cover. Different refreshments will be offered at each home and I'm hoping to partner with some of the local businesses to donate items, especially the local restaurants. It will be good for their business and good for mine.

My name is Holly Holcraft and I've been a real estate agent here in Appleby for the past ten years. We're a small mountain town with a lake and a ski resort nearby so we get visitors pretty much year round. It gives me a pretty steady business of buying and selling.

With the cookies finally in the oven and Chloe settled on the couch watching Christmas specials with Ginger and the cat-with-no-name, I buckled down to thoroughly clean up every speck of dust from my kitchen.

Hours later my house was flour free once again. Lesson learned. My knees and back were protesting and I felt an urgent need for a nap. Plus, the one two many cookie bars I had ingested were making my stomach feel unpleasant.

"Chloe, how about we go take a quick walk and get some fresh air?" I asked. Chloe immediately jumped up and ran to get her jacket. Grabbing my own jacket and the dog leash, we made our way out into the chill air.

Snow had fallen and it was beautiful. Little birds flitted through the air and spilled snow off the branches when they landed. I took a deep breath, inhaling the scent of pine trees. I laughed as Chloe imitated me, her little hands on her hips.

"It smells good Grandma," she said in her adorable little voice.

"It sure does," I responded, smiling. Ginger pulled at the leash eager to go down the road where Ben Brown lived with his dog, Bernard, a shaggy, black mutt.

Excited barking alerted me that Bernard had seen us as we approached his driveway. Ginger let out a happy whine and her tail twirled like a propeller. Ben was standing in the doorway waving to us. A warm red flannel shirt covered his portly belly and his aged jeans were tucked into a pair of brown hiking boots.

"Good morning Holly. And who is this young lady?" he asked in his deep cheery voice.

"Good to see you Ben. This is my granddaughter, Chloe. How's your new granddaughter? I see Bernard is still with you." The two dogs danced around each other with happy barks.

"She's doing well. I expect Bernard will be going home soon. I know my son misses him." Ben's daughter-in-law had just had a baby girl and Ben was watching Bernard for them. He'd also let me borrow the dog to get myself out of a scrape a few months ago.

"Speaking of going home soon. When is Alma leaving town? Now that her house is sold. I know she was planning on staying with Emmeline for the Christmas Tour of Homes but after that?" I looked at him expectantly, then realized he would be out of a job. Ben was Alma and Albert Hotchkiss's butler and I had negotiated the sale and purchase of Alma's home in the luxury estates to Emmeline Davis. Do they move with their employer? "Will you be moving with her?"

Ben gave a little shrug with his shoulders. "The plan is for them to retire to Florida after the holidays. They've already purchased a home there." He crinkled his nose. "I'm not sure I want to go. I love it here and I'm hoping maybe Emmeline will keep me on. She's going to need someone to help with that big house."

"That would be wonderful!" I exclaimed. "I love having you as a neighbor. Perhaps Emmeline would let you out more and you could join some of our community events?"

"I think I might actually enjoy doing that," he replied. "I'll let you know what happens."

"Poor Ginger is really going to miss Bernard when he leaves. Perhaps your son will bring him back to visit when your granddaughter gets a little older."

Both dogs looked up at the mention of their names. "Come along Ginger, we need to get back and get the house ready."

Planning

"Ladies, let's get started," I said tapping the clipboard I held loudly with my pen. The women were all gathered in the meeting room at my real estate office in town, conveniently located within sight of the lake and a few doors down from Mildred's candy shop, which I probably frequented too often to indulge my sweet tooth.

"We have such a short time before the event." This was putting it mildly. The Tour of Holiday Homes was only three weeks away and we had a lot of houses to decorate. Tickets were already selling like hotcakes, possibly due to a lovely article in the Gazette last month. Alma looked beautiful in the picture. Next to her were two of the women whose homes would be featured on the Tour, they were all dressed to the nine's replete with jewelry. It caused me to wonder if they dressed that way everyday.

"Emmeline, it's so good to have you on our committee this year," I said with perhaps just a tad too much enthusiasm. She was wearing a designer sweater and custom jeans that she looked awkward in. I had a feeling that Alma had volunteered her for this committee. I was beginning to realize that Alma volunteered a lot of people for things without ever volunteering herself.

She had also volunteered Emmeline to host her for Christmas this year. That has got to be a trying experience, hosting the sellers of your house, even if they are family friends. Maybe I could be a buffer between the two. Of course that would be fraught with danger if I mismanaged it. Alma had already let me have the commission from the sale and purchase of her home and the possibility of more referrals. I would have to tread lightly here. The mother in me felt sorry for Emmeline though. The poor little rich girl is a cliche, but she fit the part in every way, basically being raised by nannies.

"Patty, do you have the list of homes that have been volunteered?" Patty Bennett was a short, stocky woman in her mid forties who had helped me with the fall festival held a few weeks ago.

She stood up to speak, "Yes, Holly. We have twelve homes this year. Most of them are up in the Estates, but there are a couple in town as well." She creased her face in a frown as she said the last few words. Many of the women were not pleased that I had extended the invitation to the less luxurious homes.

Putting a smile on my face, I replied, "Thank you Patty. Have you let them all know that we will be coming by today to look through them?"

"Yes and they will all be available today as well. I don't understand why we are including homes in town?"

"Well Patty, don't you think people might appreciate Christmas decorating ideas they can actually afford?" When she didn't answer, I continued on.

"Great. As a surprise for you all, Katie of Katie May's has offered to host us all for lunch at noon. We'll do half of the houses, eat and then finish up the rest." The ladies all brightened at this news. Katie May's was the local restaurant and the food was excellent.

Cindy Gray raised her hand. I always thought her last name was pretty dour for such a perky lady. At age 72, she didn't let being short keep her from any of the fun and her blonde hair didn't have a speck of gray in it. "There won't be any dead bodies will there?" The ladies all snickered at the question, just because a few deaths happened to fall into my lap recently.

"Nope." I said the word confidently and oddly enough, Cindy looked a little disappointed. "There will be no dead bodies," I emphasized again. "This is the Christmas season, full of positivity and kindness."

We spent the next hour scheduling the order of homes and assigning them to each of the ladies. This way everyone only had a few houses to oversee. Everything was going to go perfect this time. I could just feel it.

Tour

I led the procession of cars to the first home. We were carpooling, which really made the most sense anyway. There's no point in everyone driving themselves, especially since some of the women were elderly and no longer had licenses. The road to the estates was under an overpass and looked ominous. It was dark and so deep it would almost qualify as a tunnel. Huge pine trees lined the mouth of the overpass, casting it in shadow.

Who would have guessed such a dreary road would lead to such delightful Victorian houses. Some of them even still had the old gas lights. Of course they didn't work. The Christmas Tour of Homes had been held for the past fourteen years. I'd volunteered this year to help coordinate it. Okay, well, I was volunteered. Again, by Alma. She was such a delightful lady.

At the first house, I was greeted by Alma who introduced me to her friend. Caroline Keene, a woman in her sixties wearing an immaculately tailored blue suit which failed to hide her plumpness. With her graying hair in a bun, she looked the part of an aging dowager. An exquisite crystal necklace peeked from the collar of her jacket and was sparkly enough to distract me from the arrogance she exuded.

"It's so nice to meet you Caroline," I said, extending my hand to her. "And thank you for volunteering your house this year. You were in the Gazette photo with Alma. It came out beautifully."

Caroline kept her hand firmly gripping her purse, so I lowered my own. Alma gave me an apologetic look.

"It's pronounced Carol-een," she said with a disdainful sniff, completely ignoring my comment. "I don't understand why it's so difficult to pronounce." She arched a precisely plucked eyebrow at me giving me the impression of looking down her nose at me. I had a feeling it was only Alma's presence that was keeping her civil.

"Alma, darling," she grimaced. "Is my presence going to be necessary during these preparations?" she asked as she flipped her hand through the air in our direction.

Alma looped her arm through Caroline's arm and walked her away. "Of course not sweetie. The committee will have someone assigned to your house and they will take care of everything."

"Oh, thank you Alma dear. You're so wonderful at taking care of everything. I don't understand why you're not running it yourself this year. You always do such a wonderful job." I couldn't hear anymore after that because they entered another room and the door shut behind them.

"Okay ladies. Who's the lucky winner of this house?" I asked, turning to face the group of women behind me. All but one of them avoided my gaze. They seemed to be quite experienced at that.

A tall thin woman in her 60s with gray hair down to her butt, hesitantly lifted her hand. "Uh, that would be me." She looked as if she was regretting selecting this house. In hindsight, she probably didn't actually select this house. It was more like it was thrust upon her mainly due to the lack of any other volunteers. Now I understood why.

"Laurie Culpepper right?" Not waiting for an answer, I continued on. "I know you're a real estate agent so you can dust off your people managing skills and use them on this lady." I smiled graciously at her, thankful that this was one cranky person I didn't have to deal with.

Laurie had been doing real estate here for a few years. She had come

9

here to retire. But as you know, many retirees find retired life boring and choose to work part time so she had continued to work as a real estate agent. She only did one or two transactions a year but she was a regular at all of our meetings.

Laurie gave me a crooked smile back. "Reminds me of why I wanted to quit real estate." We all laughed along with her because, hey, what else can you do?

The rest of the afternoon went along in the same general theme; homeowners grateful not to have to pay someone to put up their Christmas decorations. We went over ideas with all of the homeowners and let them know the general guidelines and our theme this year which was Grateful Giving. Most everyone opted for either a nativity scene or Santa and his reindeer.

Each house was also going to have a collection box for toys and nonperishables so we could give out Christmas baskets as well. You know, the Grateful Giving part.

Lunch was delicious as expected and the rest of the afternoon passed pleasantly.

We were all gathered in Mildred Beaumont's candy shop enjoying a cup of hot chocolate before ending the day. It was Mildred's idea really, as she pointed out, 'what could be more Christmasy than a candy shop?'

"Oh, I can't wait to see all the Santa displays," gushed Gloria. In her mid forties, she still enjoyed displaying her uniqueness through her hair color. Today it was a bright red, which looked oddly good on her. "I remember a long time ago, the Blume house used to have a wonderful display. It's such a shame they don't do it anymore."

We all gave her an odd look. "Gloria, nobody lives there anymore," pointed out Cindy, Gloria's partner in crime. If I had to describe the two of them, it would be Sophia and Rose from the Golden Girls. Cindy looked really sweet and Gloria was pretty feisty and they both had a penchant for looking for trouble.

"I know that. But that doesn't mean we can't still put on a display, does it?" she asked.

She did have a point. After all, we did have the Fall Festival there recently. It was a large house and empty. Why couldn't we end the tour there and go all out with the decorations? Santa could hand out the Christmas presents to the kids. I got more enthused as I thought about it. It worked out great for the Fall Festival, if you leave out the dead body and the bear.

"You know she does have a point. Gloria, by the way, Gloria, what is your last name?" After all these months, and I had never asked her for her last name.

"Oh, that's easy. It's Amore, like love." She put the emphasis on rolling the 'r.'

Because, of course it was, she was just that kind of person. Perhaps she has a little Blanche in her as well. "Well Gloria, why don't you check with the city and see if we can use the house? We could end the tour of homes there and have a big celebration. I'm going to put you in charge of arranging it." That ought to keep her busy. What kind of trouble could she possibly get into decorating a house for Christmas?

A little flirtation

"Are you going to the Christmas party tonight?" asked Vana Dago, fellow real estate agent and my closest friend. She was sitting next to my desk while we looked for houses for our clients.

"Looking forward to it," I replied. It was Saturday morning, which for us real estate agents is really Friday, and tonight was the annual Appleby real estate agents annual Christmas party where we all dressed up and it was always held at the Lockwood Hotel, a rather pretentious place halfway up the mountain, but the view was fantastic.

Vana was wearing a comfy sweater and jeans today and I was a little jealous as my dress was leaving me a little chilly even though I was wearing boots. It was so cold in the office, I was tempted to put my jacket back on, even if it did ruin my look. Vana was always comfortable.

"Bob's coming tonight, are you bringing Shelby?" She asked. Bob was Vana's husband. They were total opposites. She was short and slightly overweight while he was tall and thin, but they went together like bread and butter or peanut butter and jelly. Maybe like ice cream and caramel sauce. When you met them, you just knew they belonged together. Shelby White, no relation to Lucy, was another close friend of ours and one whom I had gone to school with.

"Nah, she's working and probably a good thing," I said. Shelby, had gotten us kicked out of a bar and almost kicked out of a restaurant.

She was absolutely gorgeous but had a no nonsense attitude that she sometimes took too far.

A tap at the door and both our heads swiveled to look. Omar Marroquin, another agent in the office, had his handsome head poking through the door.

"Hey, Holly, Vana. My clients were looking at your listing over on Pine Street and I was wondering if the seller was willing to offer closing costs?"

"I do believe they would consider it," I said. It was not unusual for agents to pre-negotiate like this on behalf of their clients. Often it helped to get the offer accepted the first time. Taking any other offers into consideration of course. "Why don't you submit an offer and I'll present it to them. Of course, you might want to go above the listed price a bit to adjust for however much your clients are asking for."

This was another negotiating tactic, raising the purchase price to accommodate the credit they were asking the seller to give them. It let the seller still net the same amount. Of course the final price always depends on the appraised value. No lender is going to give out more money than the house is worth.

"Will do that. Thanks Holly. Vana. Um, hey, you going to the Christmas party tonight?" And there it was, the real reason he was asking a question I knew, he knew the answer to.

"Yes, we are. I'm going with Vana." I said it quickly to dissuade him from asking me to go with him. He'd never outright asked me but he'd implied it plenty of times. "Are you going?"

"Yeah, I'll be there. See you two tonight then." His head disappeared and he pulled the door closed behind him.

Vana picked up some papers off the desk and began perusing them. "Hey, you ever consider going out with him? He's cute." She was definitely studying the paper too hard.

"Really Vana? Just the fact that you are suggesting him, tells me I should say no. You finding that ad for camo clothes interesting?" Vana was a devout animal lover and the fact that she had even picked up the advertisement alerted me that she was up to something."

"Okay fine, you got me. And definitely not. You know I would never go hunting, unless it was for berries. But really, he seems nice."

I couldn't resist making a face at the thought of going out with Omar. "I'm sorry, there's just something about him that turns me off and I believe in trusting my instincts. Let's talk about something else. Like what you're wearing tonight?"

"You know me, it's going to be something comfortable. Have you seen Travis lately?" Travis Smart was our local handsome police detective stationed in Morecroft, our closest big town, and he sometimes substituted out here for vacationing or sick deputies. Yes, our town was very small.

"Not really, since we got back from the beach. Somehow I don't think he's going to interfere in police investigations for me here in town." He had flown all the way to the beach to help us and his cousin after we found a dead body in a house that was being sold.

"That's too bad but I know he's a good guy. Just have a little patience and I know it will all work out."

I simply smiled and settled down to work. Things had been rough over the past few months and it would be nice to just be able to enjoy the holidays and not get on the bad side of the police for once.

Party time

"Oh look, it's Caroleene Keene," I said, emphasizing the pronunciation of her name. The venue at the hotel was even more beautiful than I imagined. The ballroom walls were draped with red and white chiffon and illuminated with white lights which set off the crystal chandeliers beautifully. Each table had white or red tablecloths with sprigs of pine and shiny red and gold Christmas balls

"She's a little…" began Vana, as she grabbed two glasses of champagne from a passing tray.

"Yes, she is," I finished. "Where did you meet her?" I took one of the glasses from her and took a sip. The fizziness of the champagne tickling my tongue.

"She's a real estate agent over in Morecroft. She only handles the luxury clients."

"That would explain why I haven't run into her," I said. I mean, I do handle the occasional luxury house, such as Alma's, but it's not my bread and butter. Somebody has to help the regular people find homes too and they are so much easier to deal with.

"Holly! I'm so glad you came," squealed Lucy White, our title rep, like a little girl. "Tell me all about what you and Travis have been up to." The gorgeous brunette gave me and Vana each a quick hug. "Where's Bob?"

"Oh, he's hanging out at the buffet with some of the other guys. So, yeah Holly what have you and Travis been up too?"

I gave Vana a glare. On our brief excursion to the beach, Travis had confessed his feelings for me. Unfortunately, we hadn't had much time together since we got back and, if I'm being honest, I still wasn't sure how I felt about dating seriously after all this time. Sure, the girls had set me up on dates but we all knew they weren't really going to go anywhere.

I smiled at her regretfully. "We really haven't had any time together. He's working back in Morecroft."

"Well, that's a shame," Lucy said, still smiling. "Why don't you invite him along to the real estate retreat next month? It's everybody from the industry. He'll fit right in."

"He's a cop," I said.

"I know," she said back. "Safety first. Right?"

I couldn't help it. I rolled my eyes. "I don't think we're at that point in our relationship."

"Well phooey." She stuck her bottom lip out and pouted as she said it. "Where's Shelby tonight?"

"She had to work, and I quote, 'she finds these functions rather boring.'"

"Hmph. She probably has a hot date," quipped Vana. Shelby was notorious for lusting after the guys but I actually knew the truth. Unfortunately, I couldn't tell anyone that I knew she was really a secret agent. And married. The flirting was just a cover.

"Mmmhmm," I muttered noncommittally. "We should probably mingle." Without waiting for an answer I drifted away and made my hello's to all my fellow agents. For the most part, they were all pretty decent folks. Our board was pretty good at weeding out the would be shysters.

There was some talk about Bonnie Belmar's arrest for murder and her upcoming trial in hushed whispers. I tried to stay away from those conversations and my part in it. It was odd that they were still talking about it. Laurie Culpepper looked stunning in a baby blue floor length satin gown with matching crystal jewelry.

"Wow," I said. "You are definitely rocking the sixties."

"Oh, this old thing," she said, as she mimed fanning her face. "I decided I'd come do the real estate thing tonight. It's been a while since I've been to a party."

"Why don't you come more? I know you're semi-retired, but you're still welcome."

"I know. I was just enjoying not talking about real estate, if you know what I mean."

"I do indeed and I'm looking forward to the days I don't have to talk about it." If things kept going as well as they were, maybe I would actually get to retire, now that Bonnie wasn't around to mess things up for me.

I'd finally been able to start socking money away and it felt really good to have a growing savings account. I'd even started a college fund for Chloe. You can never start too early.

Then I heard a voice that made my blood run cold. "Hello Holly. I'm sure you're just pleased as punch to see me." I turned and there she was, Bonnie Belmar in all her horrible glory. Her garish lipstick matched her bright red hair and her plump body was wrapped in a designer dress.

Now it made sense why people were whispering about her. "Yes, that's right. The judge let me out of jail. Apparently, there's a statute of limitations and it just passed. I'm a free woman. Isn't that right, Captain Moran?" The man she referred to stood next to her, dressed in a rumpled suit and smirked at me.

I was frozen. I couldn't speak. In fact, I couldn't move. *Why hadn't anyone told me?* I felt a hand on my arm pulling me away from Bonnie.

I was vaguely aware that my mouth was open.

People suddenly put themselves between the two of us and she was lost to sight. "I think it's best if we leave now," said Vana. She dragged me off to the coat check. Omar had just come in. "Hi Holly, been here long?"

"Not now Omar," we both said together. Vana bundled me into my coat and directed me out into the cold outside. The door shut behind us and silenced the voices on the other side.

I jerked to a stop. "Did you know?" I demanded.

She shook her head. "If I had I would have told you and we certainly wouldn't have come here."

"Aren't the police supposed to notify me before she's released?"

"I don't know. She didn't get convicted, so maybe not?" Her voice rose at the end. "Look Holly, it's freezing out here. Let's go home and have some hot cocoa and see what we can find out. Maybe Penny knows something." Penny Anderson is an officer at the Appleby police station who had no love for Detective William Moran. But, wait. Bonnie had called him Captain. Had that horrible little man gotten a promotion?

Shock

Vana opted to drive me home and it was probably a good thing. I had my phone out and was dialing a number before my butt even hit the car seat. "Penny? This is Holly. We just left the Christmas party and Bonnie Belmar is free?" I couldn't help it. My voice went up at the end of the sentence and ended in a shriek.

"Oh, Holly, I'm so sorry. I wanted to tell you, but Moran threatened to fire anyone who spoke up. I don't think he likes you very much."

"That's okay, Penny. Is she really free?" I just couldn't believe that any judge would let her out with the evidence against her. She had deliberately steered her car into my husband's vehicle and in the process killed one of her passengers and my beloved husband Evan along with my cat. It may be inconsequential to some people, but I loved my cat like family.

Her voice when she responded was soft with regret. "Yes. The statute of limitations expired by mere days before the charges were filed."

"Bu, but, she deliberately steered into Evan's car. It was murder." My voice quavered with outrage.

I could almost see Penny shaking her head over the phone when she responded. "There's no evidence that that happened. Again, I'm really sorry Holly."

A horrible thought suddenly struck me. "Is that why Travis is working in Morecroft?"

A long silence ensued, probably because she was trying to think of an answer. "It could be. Only the people here in the office knew."

Well that was a relief. I would hate to think that Travis would deliberately withhold that type of information from me. "Thank you Penny. I won't tell anyone what you said."

"I appreciate that Holly. Goodbye."

I don't even remember the drive home or getting into bed, everything was on automatic. My night was filled with tossing and turning so bad that Ginger and the cat-with-no-name both opted to sleep on the floor.

Thefts

"Travis, you're back," I said with just a bit too much enthusiasm. "I'd run into him at Mildred's candy shop where Chloe and I were having a cup of hot cocoa while taking a break from running errands and invited him to join us. He hung his down jacket on the back of the chair. His blue plaid button down shirt complemented his blue eyes nicely.

Having my granddaughter over was also helping to keep my mind off of Bonnie's release.

"Holly, good morning," called Mildred, proprietress of said candy store. "I've got something to tell you when you have a minute."

"Good morning Mildred, of course," I said but I was a bit distracted and antsy at the moment.

Travis had called to give me his sympathies about Bonnie as soon as he had heard but I was just glad to see him back in Appleby.

He let out a sigh that left his shoulders lower than they were before. "I'm here to investigate some thefts. I really wish Moran would hire more officers out here or make me permanent. This going back and forth is getting exhausting."

"He still hasn't hired anyone?" I wasn't actually shocked. Detective Moran, Captain Moran, I mentally corrected in my head, was the most incompetent police officer I'd ever met. The fact that he didn't like me had nothing to do with my opinion of him. Travis shook his head no.

21

"Wait, you said thefts? Is it the same people who were breaking into cabins over the summer?"

The change of subject seemed to perk him up a bit. "No. This is different. Christmas decorations have been disappearing. It's probably just some kids having fun. Although, Alex MacGregor's house was broken into and he didn't have any decorations up yet."

Mildred brought him a hot cup of coffee and a muffin without being asked.

"My complements," she said as she set them on the table.

"I'm sorry to hear that, was anything taken?" I asked as he bit into the pumpkin muffin.

He shrugged his shoulders. "Not that Alex could tell. He was mostly disturbed by the whole thing."

"I hope you catch them. We're decorating for the Christmas Tour of Homes and I'd hate to see them mess that up. It's such a great event for charity."

"I definitely plan on it. It's nice to see you again Chloe," He said, addressing my granddaughter. "I see you're out shopping with your grandma." It was hard to miss the multiple shopping bags currently resting at our feet.

"It's nice to see you. I'm trying to talk Nana into taking me ice skating but she says she's too old." Chloe put a scowl on her face as she said this.

I pursed my lips while she said this and then transformed it into a smile when Travis directed his gaze my way.

"I don't think she looks too old," he said. "I think you just need to work on her a little harder. I have a feeling she'll give in." He grinned and looked at me while he said it, his blue eyes twinkling under his tousled brown hair, his eyes locked on mine.

"Thanks a lot Detective Smart. Perhaps you should come skating too."

"Oh yes, please?" cried Chloe. "Then when Nana falls you can pick her up."

"Wow Chloe. I have no intention of falling or requiring assistance. I think I can handle a pair of skates," I said.

"Yay," said Chloe. "We're going skating!" I shook my head at how easily I had fallen into her trap. She was just a wee bit too smart for her own good."

I looked at Travis who was trying, and failing, not to laugh. "Are you coming? There might be criminals there," I suggested.

"I guess I should go check that out. Just to be thorough in my search you know." We finished our food and then he helped us with our jackets, then escorted us to the door.

I waved goodbye to Mildred as we exited the shop and she gave me an exasperated look. Too late, I remembered she wanted to tell me something. I gave her an apologetic look and mouthed that I would be back through the window. I don't think she believed me.

Needless to say, I fell on the ice. Perhaps more than once. I guess, I'm not as good as I once was. Or it could have been because it was so pleasant to have Travis help me up. Yeah, I'm gonna go with that one. Chloe had found it all to be hilariously funny.

We were now all enjoying a delicious cup of hot cocoa from a lakeside stand. We brushed snow off of a bench and sat down so we could enjoy the view. Sunlight made the snow glisten.

Behind us, kids were laughing as they skated around the frozen section of the lake that was cordoned off for their use. It was a shame they'd had to miss out on the first month of skating due to Pete MacGregor's unfortunate demise but they were making up for lost time now.

"Holly!" called out a musical voice and I turned smiling.

"I recognize that voice," I said. "Toni and Mori, how delightful to see you!" Toni and Mori Makimoto had purchased a lovely Tudor house over the summer so they could spend more time with their families. They looked so cute bundled up in matching jackets and hats. "How are you enjoying Appleby in the winter?"

"Our children and their kids are loving the snow," said Toni. "They are currently on the ice rink. I think my daughter has only fallen four times."

"Yes," said Mori. "Quite the improvement over yesterday."

"I'm so glad we ran into you and Officer Smart. I was just wondering if you had found our Santa Claus?" She asked, looking at Travis.

"Santa Claus?" I asked frowning.

"Yeah, I told you about the thefts I was investigating," he said to me. Turning back to the Makimoto's he continued. "Not yet. I am still looking though. And you aren't the only one. I've had three reports of Santas going missing and two of Baby Jesus."

"Wait, what?" I laughed. "Someone is stealing Baby Jesus and Santa Claus?"

"Yes," said the Makimoto's together. "Our poor reindeer are all alone on the roof now, since Santa is missing," continued Toni. "It wouldn't be so bad, but it was from a set my mother had from the forties carved from wood."

"Wow." I shook my head in disbelief. "I've seen a lot of weird stuff but this really takes the cake. Missing Santa and Baby Jesus."

"Who would steal Santa?" piped up Chloe with big eyes. "Does that mean we won't get any presents this year?"

"Oh don't you worry honey," said a smiling Toni as she bent down to address Chloe. "They're not the real Santa. He's still up at the North Pole getting the presents ready with the elves." Chloe breathed a sigh of relief and when Toni straightened back up I mouthed 'thank you' to her.

"Well Detective Smart, are you going to break this case?" I asked.

"I sure plan on it," he replied with a grin which only made my heart beat faster.

"In that case, Toni and I will collect our kids and let you get to work. We have hot chocolate and cookies waiting for us at home," declared Mori, the chef in the family.

"Tell me about these thefts," I said to Travis as we walked to the car, Chloe between us, holding both our hands.

"There's not much to go on. The missing Santa's were between three and four feet tall. The baby Jesus' were three to six inches and had the manger attached."

"Do you think that's significant? The manger I mean."

Travis shrugged. "I don't know. I mean the whole thing is weird to begin with. It just sounds like kids having a lark."

"They're not going to get any presents and Santa is going to put them on the naughty list," said Chloe sadly.

Travis gave her a most beautiful smile. "Don't you worry, I'm going to catch them." He looked over at me with a wistful look on his face. "She makes me miss having a kid of my own.

The comment made my heart hurt. I mean sure, he could still have kids but at our age, it would be really hard. What with a baby waking up at all hours and the nervous waiting when they're sick. Chloe's four and sometimes it's really tough recovering from a day of activity with her. I don't know how I ever managed when I was younger.

Plus he would never have grand kids. I couldn't imagine not having my Chloe. Who does he have? Does he have parents or siblings? I really don't know much about him outside of his police work here.

His voice interrupted my thoughts. "You're frowning."

"I am? Sorry, I was just thinking. I couldn't imagine not having my kids or grandkids. I'm sorry, you never got to experience that."

"It's okay, I've come to terms with it. I volunteer a lot at the schools and I've been a big brother for years now."

Wow. I really didn't know anything about him. "We need to talk,"

I said seriously, possibly too seriously because his brow suddenly furrowed.

"Talk?"

"Yes. As in, have a proper date and really get to know each other."

He sighed audibly and relaxed. "You're right. That's exactly what we should do. How about Tipsy's tomorrow night at six?"

"You should go Nana," said Chloe, looking up at me with a smile on her little face.

"I guess it's two to one. I will meet you there," I said.

Travis cocked an eyebrow at me. "Hmm, you're not meeting me there because you want to leave quickly in case it's a bad date do you?"

"That wouldn't really work, would it? I think you know where I live."

"Yes, yes I do. So, I'll see you tomorrow night. At six p.m. sharp. I know how real estate agents are."

"I will do my best to be on time but if I am late, which I'm sure I won't be, I give you permission to start with a drink."

I gave him a wink and we said our goodbyes.

Chloe tugged on my skirt as we walked away. "I think I like him," she whispered as I leaned over to her. I think I liked him too I thought with a smile that wouldn't leave my face.

Did You Hear?

I was sound asleep, lost in my dreams, when I was rudely interrupted by the jangling of my phone. Ginger groaned in her sleep and then went back to snoring. The cat, who still didn't have a name, stretched and then snuggled against Ginger's chest.

I fumbled for my phone on the nightstand and thumbed the answer button.

"Hello? Holly? It's Gloria. We've got a murder to solve." Gloria sounded deliriously happy.

"Gloria, don't sound so happy when you say it," came Cindy's voice over the line admonishing her.

"Gloria? Is that Cindy with you? Why are you calling me so late? Who died?" I asked.

"They found Laurie Culpepper frozen in the snow," she exclaimed.

"You mean like poor Pete?" said Maggs.

"Yes, and Pete was murdered, you know," she said to someone else.

"Am I on speaker phone?" I asked.

"Yes. It's the book club ladies, we're all here together."

"She was just at the Christmas meeting with us," said yet another voice. "I just can't believe it."

I took my phone away from my ear and looked at the time. "Gloria it's two a.m. in the morning. What are you all doing together?"

"Well you see, I had been out late with Joanne (that would be the receptionist at the police station) and she got a call from Penny that Laurie had been found frozen in the snow. So of course I had to let Cindy know and she was having a Pinochle game at Mildred's house with Maggs. Oh, it was simply too convenient. We're all here now."

She finally ran down and I waited for her to continue.

"Holly, are you there?" she finally asked.

"Yes. I was waiting for you."

"Don't wait for me, come join us."

"Join you where?" I asked exasperated.

"At Mildred's. We're just around the corner. Or we could come to your house?" Ugh, I really didn't want to go out in the snow. Of course, if they came here I wouldn't have to get dressed. I should be ashamed of myself, asking old ladies to go out in the snow when I didn't even want to.

"I'll come down there. Just give me five minutes," I finally muttered, swinging my legs over the side of the bed and grabbing my robe from the closet.

"It's fine. Just open the door, we're right outside," said Gloria as someone began knocking. Ginger didn't even budge.

"Great dog you are," I hissed at her. "Intruders could be outside and you're just snoozing on."

Ginger opened one brown eye to look at me and then closed it again and started snoring. I left the two animals asleep on my bed and went to answer the door.

Maggs was standing on the doorstep panting. Her six foot frame wrapped in a man's jacket, snow pants and boots. "Took you long enough. You gonna invite me in or do I have to freeze to death out here first?"

"Come in." I looked past her to the empty walkway.

"The rest are coming. They apparently like the cold more than I do." Sure enough, Gloria was just coming around the corner of the garage and Cindy and Mildred were right behind her.

"Go straight into the kitchen and get something hot to drink," I said. If they were going to show up at 2 in the morning, then they could very well make their own drinks.

Mildred hustled past me into the kitchen. My quiet retreat that I love so much, was seriously lacking in the charm department at this early hour. "You ladies go sit down and get Holly up to speed. Laurie was our friend and we need to find out who killed her."

As we all settled on the sofa, Ginger leisurely strolled into the living room, stretching her back legs one by one, then making the rounds to get her ears scratched. She retired once again back to the bedroom and, I assumed, onto the bed.

"I really can't believe she's gone," I said. "I just saw her at the company Christmas party."

"Ooh, I heard Bonnie was there," said Cindy.

I pressed my lips together in a thin line and felt my shoulders tighten. "Now, now girls," said Mildred bustling out with a tray of hot cocoa topped with marshmallows. "Let's not get Holly upset right now. We need her brain power at full capacity."

Like that was gonna happen at two a.m. Right. I took a few deep breaths before speaking. "Now ladies. Why do you think Laurie was murdered? Did the police say her death was suspicious?"

Glances were cast among the ladies before Mildred finally spoke again. "Not exactly. But I know Laurie and she would never have gone out in the cold for a walk. She hates it just as much as Maggs does."

"Joanne said Penny told her that she was found a few blocks from her house. She had her snow boots on. It looked like she just went for a walk."

"Maybe she did," I said. "The weather has been beautiful."

"I told you, she hated the cold weather. It has to be something else," pointed out Mildred.

29

I took a deep breath and blew it out slowly through my lips. An annoying little irritation began building between my shoulder blades. I twisted my shoulders and took another deep breath. "Were there any signs of foul play?" I finally asked as they all looked at me expectantly.

Gloria scrunched her face and shoulders, "Welp," she began drawing out the word. "Not exactly."

"Not exactly or no?" I fixed her squirming body with a stare.

Cindy lifted her hand in the air. "Um, the police said it looked like she slipped and fell, hitting her head and knocking her out and then she froze."

"Hmm," I said. A funny feeling tickled my brain.

"Hmm, what?" asked Maggs.

Ignoring her question instead I asked another. "What time did this occur?"

"Oh, oh, Joanne said it must have been late this afternoon. Around three p.m." jumped in Cindy. Gloria glared at her because, of course, that was her news to tell.

"She fell at three p.m. and no one saw her lying there in the snow?"

Maggs made a face and bobbed her head back and forth. "There are hedges lining the road where she lives and she was behind them."

I threw my hands up in frustration. "Everything you are telling me justifies the position of the police that it was an accident. Why are we all sitting here at," I paused to check the clock, "now 3 a.m. Can anyone tell me why this is possibly suspicious? Besides, she hated the cold." I added at the last second.

The ladies looked at each other and then the floor. Gloria turned to Maggs. "Well we gave it a shot. It was fifty-fifty." She raised her hands in a shrug and then dropped them.

Mildred gave me a disapproving look. "Really, Holly, I expected more from you."

I pressed my fingertips to my forehead and then dropped my hands.

"Ok, I will look into it tomorrow, if you'll let me go back to sleep now."

The ladies glanced at each other again.

"What?"

"It's just that we were hoping you would go take a look now," said Cindy.

"Now?"

"Yes," said Maggs. "Important evidence could be gone tomorrow."

I closed my eyes and shook my head. Opening them again, I asked, "Won't the area be taped off by the police?"

"Oh, no. Penny told Joanne that Moran declared it was an accident and that's that."

Realizing they weren't going to let me go back to sleep, I conceded the point and left to get dressed.

Ten minutes later and fully dressed in warm clothes and boots I looked at Ginger sleeping comfortably on the bed. "Nope, no more snoozing for you. If I have to go out, you're coming with me." I'd wished I had my dog with me on more than one occasion recently. Ginger looked at me with what I can only describe as shock and then she slowly staggered off the bed and slowly stretched one back leg and then the other.

"Yeah, me too," I said.

We all piled into my car and Gloria's and Maggs directed me to Laurie's house. She lived at the edge of town, the last house on the street. "Nice location. Close enough for neighbors but still a bit secluded," I observed.

We got out and walked quietly to the location where she was found. It was located a block away from the neighborhood. True there was a hedge, but still, someone should have seen her. A child, a dog. If it was foul play, how had no one noticed her getting hit over the head?

The street was quiet when we arrived and the silence pressed on the ladies so that they communicated by whisper. The old snow was hard and crunchy underfoot from thawing and refreezing. I was more likely to slip here than I had been on the ice rink. The police had trampled the snow all around the area so there were no footprints. "Great job Moran," I muttered.

The tree line came down close to the road right here. I looked around at the neighborhood. I'd sold a home here a few years ago. The houses were all tucked up tight and there were no lights on. Not unexpected at nearly 4 in the morning. The only sound was Ginger's feet as she'd pick up one snowbooted paw and then another to shake them.

The ladies were following closely behind me and they all jumped when I turned suddenly to face them.

"How do they know she died at three?"

"I, I don't know," stuttered Maggs.

I raised my eyebrows at her. "You need to find that out. The cold can alter timelines. Did she have any enemies?" At the blank stares, I continued. "Mildred, that's your job. You and Cindy can ask around."

"What about me?" asked Gloria, not wanting to be left out.

"You are going to be busy getting the Blume house set up for Christmas. You won't have any time for investigations."

The crestfallen look on her face was small solace for rousting me from my bed in the middle of the night.

I let Ginger's lead out and let her sniff around the area. You never know, she might pick something up. She sniffed around the area where the body was and then headed over and sniffed around the treeline. After a few minutes she came back to me and looked up ready to go.

I was ready to go too. I dropped the ladies off at Mildred's and went home, peeling off my clothes and then dropping into bed. I was asleep before Ginger.

Pets

"Your fur is cold," meowed the tiny black cat, sniffing Ginger's fur.

"It was cold outside, snow everywhere," woofed Ginger quietly. Holly was already snoring beside them.

The cat snuggled into Ginger's fur to warm her and began purring loudly. "What did you see?" she asked.

"We drove in the car with the ladies and then stopped outside a house. Holly let me sniff around. There was a dead body there earlier. I think maybe I met her once? I recorded all the smells but I don't know what Holly was looking for. I don't think she did either."

In fact, Ginger had sniffed and sorted the smells into different categories. She was pretty sure Holly wasn't interested in the raccoon that had raided the trash can or the bear that had crept up close through the trees. Multiple people had been there recently, she'd smelled the asphalt on their shoes and the coffee cups in the trash can. Someone had been standing in the trees, their scent evident where they had leaned against the tree. The dead woman's blood had leaked through the snow and was still fairly strong. The other scents were barely there.

Holly mumbled in her sleep and the dog and cat snuggled deeper into the covers and dozed off.

Problems

I woke up late in the morning or would that be later? The sun was already streaming through my window when I finally opened my eyes. Still groggy, I grabbed my robe and padded into the kitchen for coffee. It was getting harder each year to bounce back from lack of sleep. Aging is a real killer.

I sat sipping my coffee at the island, watching the sun sparkle off the wine glasses suspended upside down under the cabinets and wishing I had spent more time with Laurie.

Of course, nobody had known it would be the last time. That's the problem sometimes, the missed opportunity that you didn't take. The what ifs. What if I had picked up the cat from the vet instead of my husband. Would he be here with me now instead of dying in a car accident?

That's when Travis popped into my head. Actually, he'd been popping into my head more frequently. I found myself hoping to run into him whenever I ran into town. Butterflies tickled my tummy at the thought of seeing his beautiful blue eyes that seemed to bore into my soul.

What was really holding me back was the fact that we had both lost our spouses in the same accident. Could you really build a relationship based on a loss or would it perpetually haunt us?

The butterflies danced faster as I thought about our date tonight. The date I would definitely NOT be late to.

My phone rang and I picked it up to see it was my assistant Joe Marvel. He was currently studying to get his real estate license. I already considered him indispensable, being licensed he could help out even more.

Thinking of Joe made me think of his sister, Sam. She ran some escape rooms in Morecroft. Would an escape room be an appropriate date? I mean it's fairly neutral, no expectations, no food to spill on myself. Maybe we could double date with Vana and her husband.

"Holly? Are you there?"

"Yes, Joe. I'm sorry. It was a late night and I'm still a bit sleepy. What's up?"

"Tom Frank called and wants you to call back right away. He said it's really important." I had only listed his house two weeks ago and couldn't imagine what could be so urgent.

"Okay, how's the studying going?"

"I'm plodding through. Do you actually use any of this information in work?"

I laughed. "Not really. It's basically background information. The joke is that nothing you learn for the test is really real world information. It's like the foundation. I mean, you need to know it, but it's not going to help with your career."

"Ugh. Well, then I'm going to get the highest score just to annoy them."

"Sorry Joe, but they don't give scores. You pass or don't pass."

I could almost feel his angst over the phone. Everyone goes through it. The test is hard but I knew he would do a great job.

"That's a little disappointing but at least I only have to take it once. I'll see you at the office."

He disconnected and I got back to finishing my coffee. The kitten jumped up on the counter and rubbed against my arms. "I still need a name for you don't I?" I asked as I rubbed the top of her forehead with my finger.

The vet had told me she was a girl and she was a year old. I don't know why I continued to refer to her as a kitten when technically she was an adult but she was just so tiny.

"How about Blackie?" She sat down and began to wash her face with her front paws.

"Midnight?" The hindfoot went up in the air and the cleaning continued.

"Sassy? Ebony? Every suggestion was met with being ignored. "Fine then, what do you want to be called?" She looked up at me and meowed as if she could understand and then came over and rubbed her head up against my chin, having to rise on her hind legs to do so.

"You sure are a friendly kitten," I said. She looked straight in my face and meowed again. I cocked my head at her like Ginger does to me. "Friendly? Is that it?"

She meowed again and butted my arm. Just to test her I said, "Max" and she actually hissed at me. "Friendly?" I said again and she rubbed up against me purring.

Now if that isn't the strangest name for a cat ever, but I can't keep calling her kitten, so Friendly it is.

Now that that was decided I picked up my phone and called Tom. His gravelly voice coming clearly over the line.

"Hey Holly, thanks for returning my call so quickly. So just to get right into it…I'd like to raise the price on my house."

My mouth dropped open. "You want me to raise the price?"

"Well yeah, prices are going up. We should take advantage of that."

"Bu…but it's been on the market for two weeks with no offers. We need to lower the price or you're never going to sell."

"Maybe they just think it's not worth the value because it's priced too low?" His voice rose at the end of the sentence as if doubting what he was saying.

I tried to contain my laughter. It wouldn't due to offend my client no matter how stupid they were acting.

"We are not raising the price. You hired me for my expertise to get your house sold and now you need to let me do my job. In 25 years of real estate a house that's not selling has never been sold by raising the price. Furthermore, it's the middle of winter. Sales are slow at this time of year."

There was silence and then, "Well, if you're sure. I guess I could wait longer."

I could tell by his voice that he didn't want to wait longer. "That's probably best. Two weeks and we'll see if anything changes and then I promise, we will reevaluate it."

Crises averted, I took a long hot shower and then got dressed for the office.

My phone rang on my drive into town and I clicked the answer button on my console. It was a number I didn't recognize.

"Holly? This is Candace Whitford. We bought the Oates's house?"

My mind wandered over a dozen thoughts as I wondered what the buyers of Carol's house could possibly want. It's never good when a buyer calls up the seller's agent. Then my heart rose. Maybe she loved my work and wanted to recommend someone to me.

"Yes, this is Holly, how can I help you?" I said cheerfully.

Candace let out a deep sigh over the phone and my heart sank. "Someone dug a big hole in our backyard. My husband and I went away for a few days and we came back to find it. Do you have any idea why someone would have done such a thing?"

My eyebrows raised of their own accord and I pursed my lips as I thought over what she just said. "I really can't. How big of a hole is it?" I asked, puzzled.

"It's six feet long and four feet deep." I could hear a little tremble in her voice. "You don't think…"

I smiled before responding, hoping it would carry through my voice. "I don't think so. There was a broken water pipe in the backyard that washed a bunch of animal bones into the neighbors yard and the police were all over that place. They would have certainly found..," I didn't want to say 'body' out loud, "...anything, if there was anything to find," I continued. "We did disclose all of this in the paperwork."

"Yes, yes, you did. I just have no idea what anyone could have been looking for? Did the previous owners live here for very long?" The worry in her voice was very evident even over the phone.

"Candace, I'm sure it's nothing to worry about. Would you send me a picture of the hole? Maybe someone was looking for the septic at the wrong house," I said in a moment of brilliant inspiration.

"Oh, yeah, maybe. I'll send you the picture. Thank you." The line went dead and a moment later my phone dinged as the picture came through. Dug down through the snow, it clearly looked like a place where a body had been buried. The edges weren't even and there were piles of dirt scattered here and there as if someone had dug up something in a hurry. I decided it couldn't hurt to stop by and take a look, maybe give her some more reassurance. I turned my car around and headed back up the hill.

Police Report

One look at the hole and I knew the police had to be called. It was way too body-like to be anything else. The weird thing was small flakes of red coating the ground. They almost looked like thin slivers of plastic like the coating on a Christmas ball that gets wet and the color flakes off.

Candace stood on the other side dressed in jeans and a large gray coat; her arms hugging her body and her eyes alternating between me and the hole. Her brown hair was done up in a sloppy bun.

"What do you think?" Her brow was furrowed with anxiety. "Gloria told me that you investigate...things." She couldn't quite bring herself to say 'murders' which is most likely what Gloria said I do. Gloria was the girlfriend of the first victim whose case I reluctantly solved to clear my client, Carol, who was the previous owner of this house.

That thought made me think of Jacob Martin. Jacob who desperately wanted to buy Carol's house but somehow missed out on it twice. He had then purchased a house just around the corner and up the hill a bit. Biting my lower lip, I wondered if he could see Candace's backyard from his balcony. Is that why he moved there?

"Holly?!" Her yell made me realize I had neglected to answer her question.

"I think if it was a body, there would probably be bugs and worms here also and there aren't." Confidence tinged my words as I said them.

It made sense to me. "And look at those little flakes on the ground. That wouldn't be from a body. Somebody possibly had a treasure box stashed here and then dug it up. You know how people bury time capsules and things. I'm sure that's all it was. Still, someone did trespass on your property so you should probably make a police report just to be safe."

Candace had visibly relaxed at my words but now tensed up again. Seeing her reaction I added, "Not to worry, it's just to protect you in case they are stupid enough to injure themselves. I would also recommend getting a dog. Reformed criminals have reported that they won't target homes with dogs. Have you seen anyone strange around your property?"

She shook her head. "Oh, a man came by asking if we needed yard work done. Let me see, that was right before we left for vacation."

"Can you describe him?"

"He was a little old to be looking for yard work, maybe early forties? I don't know, it was weeks ago."

I retrieved my phone from my purse and looked at her. She gave a small nod and I called the police dispatch where I gave Joanne Davidson all the information and she assured me, someone would be there shortly.

We retired back into her house to await their arrival. "I love what you've done with the place," I said as I admired her decor. Contrary to Carol's somewhat hodge-podge way of decorating, Candace's house looked like it came from the pages of a fashion magazine.

"Thank you," she said humbly. "I used to be an interior designer, but decided to retire and enjoy the mountains." My eyebrows rose, as she couldn't possibly be of retirement age. "I see that look. I've made some good investments so I was able to retire early. My husband Alan and I like to travel and we do volunteer work to stay busy.

"Perhaps you will. The problem is getting them to stay year-round." A sudden thought struck me. "Hey, if you would really like to get to know the locals, you should join the Holiday Tour of Homes committee. There's not a lot of men on it." I thought for a moment and frowned. "Okay, there's no men on it, but the women are a hoot. Maybe if your husband joins, we'll get some men," I added cheerfully.

A knock at the door interrupted us as she went to answer it. My heart dropped at the sight of the officer standing there.

"Not who you were expecting Mrs. Holcraft?" sneered Captain William Moran. As a detective he was dressed in plainclothes; rumpled, ill-fitting clothes as usual. He never seemed to take pleasure in his appearance. Some people get promoted because they do a good job and some people because they are rude and obnoxious and it's easier to just give them what they want. The latter was Captain Moran.

"Nice to see you too Bill." Nice would be if I could stuff him and Bonnie in a bag and drop them in the lake.

Candace read the room and headed him off before he entered the house. "Hello, Captain Moran," she squinted as she read his name tag. "My name is Candace Whitford. Why don't we go around to the back," she said, motioning toward the side gate. He gave her a smile, which was more like a leer, as he appraised her figure.

Stepping aside, he motioned for her to show the way. I'm pretty sure he was checking out her backside as she walked away. "Oh, no need for you to come Mrs. Holcraft, I can take it from here."

Candace is a smart woman, she immediately jumped in with, "oh, no Holly, please stay. I could really use your support right now," said in a slightly quavering voice.

I mugged a look at the Captain's back. "Of course, Candace, whatever you need," I said smugly. Moran just 'hmphed' and went to look at the hole. He walked around it a few times, basically putting on a show.

"So what do you think, detective?" asked Candace with a worried look.

Moran crossed his arms and supported his chin with his right hand.

Call me Bill, please. "It's hard to say. Looks like some kids were up to mischief."

"Mischief?" she questioned.

"Yeah, you know, let's scare the new neighbor. That kind of mischief. I wouldn't worry too much about it. But, if it would make you feel better, I could have the patrols drive by your house to make sure there's no more trouble." Sure, he would. More likely, he would be the patrol.

Candace smiled sweetly at him. "That would be wonderful. Thank you."

"Well, he's worthless," she said as we watched him drive away from her front porch.

I gave a snort of laughter. "You've got him pegged. But I must say, you handled him wonderfully."

"You learn to deal with all sorts of people when you do home decor. It seems to bring out the crazies."

"Wow," I said. "It sounds just like real estate." That was our bonding moment. I just hoped she didn't end up being a crazy psycho murderer.

My phone rang again as I drove away from the house. "This is Holly."

"Oh Holly, thank goodness," said Cindy. "I'm at Joe Pinkerton's house and someone stole Santa right off the roof!"

"Are you sure?"

"Of course I'm sure. There's no Santa! What do I do? Am I going to get fired?"

"Cindy, it's okay. You're not going to get fired. No one fires volunteers. I need you to call the police and make a report. Text me a description of the missing Santa and I'll see if I can find a replacement."

"Of course. I should have done that right away. I didn't even think of it."

"It's okay Cindy, just do it now. I'll check up on you later."

My phone rang again at the bottom of the hill. "Hey Lucy what's up?"

"Holly you are not going to believe this. Someone broke into Chester

Pembroke's house while they were at church and stole baby Jesus from the nativity scene. Can you believe that?"

I groaned inside. "Just the baby Jesus?"

"Yes. Why on earth would someone do that?"

"You're going to need to call the police and make a report. There's been a series of thefts going on. Travis is already investigating it."

"Really? I hadn't heard. I'll do that right now. Thanks Holly."

I disconnected. What was going on? This theft business definitely took priority over poor Laurie, who may or may not have been killed.

Photographs

fter Lucy's phone call, I barely registered the beautiful snow covered trees, my mind wondering what was wrong with people? I mean this is the holiday season and someone is stealing, someone may have committed murder and someone is now digging random holes in people's backyards.

Feeling the need for some hot consolation, I stopped off at Mildred's candy shop for a hot cocoa. The door bell tinkled as I pushed through into the warmth and delicious smells of candy. Patty Bennett was at the counter conferring with Mildred and Maggs.

"Oh, Holly, come look. Patty has pictures from the Christmas party," called Mildred.

Patty handed me her phone and I looked through the photographs. There was poor Laurie dressed in her gorgeous blue satin gown with the lovely blue necklace and matching earrings. She really looked fantastic and there was a pang in my heart that she wouldn't get to enjoy another one. Snow is not a very forgiving mistress; even more so for the elderly. Although, come to think about it, she wasn't that much older than me.

"It's so sad about Laurie," said Patty. "She was such a lovely woman. She helped me find my house, you know."

"I didn't know that. I'm so sorry she's gone," I said.

Mildred patted her hand in sympathy. "That's why we need to be extra careful in the snow. At our age, it's too easy to slip and fall."

Patty picked up her foot. "That's why I wear soccer cleats." Sure enough, the bottom of her shoe was covered with tiny round studs. Both Mildred's and my eyebrows rose.

"Won't that damage the floors?" asked Mildred, worriedly glancing at her tile floor.

"Naw, they're rubber tipped," she said as she slipped her shoe back on.

"Any news from the police about Laurie?" I asked, while scanning the fresh fudge in the case. Not that I needed it but it really, really smelled good and my declining attitude needed a chocolate boost.

Mildred shook her head sadly. "No. Moran classified it as an accident and that's it for any investigation. "I'm going to go by and pick up her belongings from the mortuary later today. Her son lives out of the country and he's having a hard time getting back here. I told him I would take care of things until he could arrive."

I gave her a sympathetic look. "That's very kind of you. Let me know if I can help in any way."

"Funny you should say that," she said. "Would you go with me to pick up her belongings? She's at the mortuary in Morecroft." Mildred fixed me with a sad look and waited for my answer.

"Of course Mildred. As long as you throw in some vanilla nut fudges." I gave her my own sad look back. Two could play at that game.

"Of course dear. As long as you drive. Patty, would you like to come too?"

Patty gave an emphatic, "no," as she put her phone in her purse and backed away toward the door. Maggs had already beaten her to it. "I've got *sooo* much stuff to do today. I'm going to be so terribly busy. Way too busy." She pushed the door open with her backside and ducked through to the outside.

Mildred waited for the door to swing shut, blocking out the cold wind before speaking. "Too busy watching 'The Price is Right,' I'm sure." She put six pieces of fudge into a small box and handed it to me. "Be here at five."

An Offer

I left the candy shop and walked back down the sidewalk to my office. Two pieces of fudge later and I was ready to take on the world.

Joe opened my office door as I reached for the lock with my key in hand.

"Nice to see you've made it here in once piece," he quipped. "You'll be happy to note an offer came in on Tom Frank's place in your email. I printed it and put it on your desk."

"Thank you Joe. Have I ever told you you're the best?"

""You could say it again, I wouldn't complain," he snarked.

"Get to work," I joked back. With my coat and purse dispensed with on the hooks behind the door, I settled behind my desk to peruse the new offer. My shoulders tightened uncomfortably and I shifted on the chair. Tom wasn't going to like this offer and I didn't relish calling him.

He answered on the second ring. "Well, Tom, I received an offer on your property," I said quickly to get it over with. Waiting for his response, I found myself gritting my teeth.

"Great! What is it? Wait, I can tell by your silence that I didn't get what I wanted." His frown came clearly through the phone. Taking a big breath, I began.

"It's $5,000 below your original asking price. I could counter back at the original price if you want."

"I'll take it."

"You'll what?" I asked in astonishment. I figured there was going to be a royal battle to get him to accept this offer. The only offer in two weeks. "But this morning, you just said…"

"I said, I'll take it," he said cutting me off. Strangely enough it sounded like he was smiling. "My grandchild was just born and I'm going to move closer to my son and daughter-in-law. Family is more important than a house you know." He was actually admonishing me. For a moment there was nothing I could say, then I found my voice.

"You are so right. I will get the offer sent over to you in a few moments and we'll get this done." How quickly things could change in an hour. After disconnecting the call, I docusigned the offer to him as quickly as I could. There was no point in letting him get cold feet.

I worked on things in the office until 4:30 and then started wrapping it up so I could meet Mildred at five. It wouldn't do to let her have an excuse to pick on me for being late. Can I help it? I am a real estate agent after all.

Mortuary

Mildred already had the shop locked up by the time I swung by with two minutes to spare. The drive to Morecroft went by fairly quickly. As we pulled up to the Mortuary, which was a repurposed house, I remembered my date with Travis.

"Is something wrong?" asked Mildred. "You look like you ate a lemon."

I gritted my teeth together. "I have a date tonight with Travis," I explained.

"Is that a bad thing?" she asked.

"No. But I'm supposed to be there at six."

"Oh. Well, this should be quick. I mean, we're just picking up her belongings. How long could that take?"

I shrugged.

"It'll be fine," she continued. "And it's not like you're covered in mud or anything. You look good."

That was definitely true. I was wearing my business clothes and he had seen me covered in mud when I rescued Jerry Oates from a murderer. "You're right. It'll be fine," I said.

We walked into the front lobby which used to be a living room. The smell of antiseptic assailed my nose as we entered. Filing cabinets lined two walls and a desk with the nameplate, Dr. Daniel Whitby gracing it, was situated in front of a third wall facing the door. We rang the little bell on the desk and a few moments later the mortician appeared from a door on the left. He was an older gentleman. The white scrubs he wore were tight around the middle and he wasn't going to be winning any hair competitions anytime soon. A few stray hairs poked out from beneath the white surgical cap and he pulled off his gloves as he spoke to us.

"Good to see you again, Mildred," he said, walking behind the desk.

"Good to see you again too, Dr. Whitby." Mildred was positively beaming as she spoke his name.

"Yes. I have your friend's items right here. If you could just sign this release for me." He handed her a clipboard and she signed at the bottom of the paper clipped to it. He then handed her a large plastic bag containing the items Laurie had been wearing when she died.

"Is there anything else I can do for you?" he asked.

"No dear, this is just fine. Thank you for taking care of her."

Dr. Whitby smiled back at Mildred, leading me to suspect there was more going on behind the scenes. "It is my job. Feel free to call me if you need anything else." He waited a moment longer and then stepped back through the door and out of sight.

Mildred turned and led the way back out the door and down the steps to the car.

"Such a charming place," she said as I stared at her. "What?"

"Is there something going on between you too?"

Mildred actually blushed. "Don't be silly, I've known Dan since elementary school."

"Mmhmm," I responded. "Won't we need to pick out an outfit for her burial?"

"Yes, I'll have to bring it by later. I wanted to ask the ladies their opinion on it," said Mildred.

I grinned. "I guess that means another visit to Daniel huh?" I said and raised my eyebrows.

Mildred just smiled and tossed her head as she got into the car.

We drove along in silence for a few miles. The sun had gone down and my headlights illuminated the snow on the side of the road, making it glow. Here and there Christmas lights shone through the trees. I tried not to think about my impending date. I had tried not to think about it all day, which is why I forgot about it. Every time I thought about dinner tonight, butterflies would roost in my belly.

I don't know why I was so nervous. It's not like I'd never been alone with Travis before. Of course all the previous times had involved me trying to solve a murder or prevent a murder and he hadn't always looked fondly at my involvement.

Things had changed on our little excursion to the beach when he had come out to help me solve a murder. Travis had said the most romantic words to me, "yes, I am going to interfere in police business for you." And he had, and it had been wonderful working with him, I just hoped that being home wouldn't pit us on opposite sides again.

I stopped in front of Mildred's car at the candy store, to let her out. She got out of the car still with a smile on her face. As she moved to close the door, I leaned over suddenly, "Mildred, you had something to tell me?"

She pressed her lips together. "I'll talk to you later, you've got a date to get ready for. Now get going." She shut the door and I pulled out of her driveway. She smiled at me but her face didn't look happy anymore.

Date Night

I'm quite proud of the fact that I arrived at Tipsy's right on time. I could see Travis through the window, dressed in a blue flannel shirt and dark blue jeans that looked like they were custom made for his body. A quiver ran through me like a flock of butterflies taking off. He saw me and held the door open. "Nice to see you right on time."

"I'm on time, sometimes, when it's really important."

The waitress led us to a quiet booth in the back with a candle flickering on the white table cloth. Travis helped me as I shrugged off my coat.

"Any news on your investigation?" I asked, settling into my seat.

"It's so crazy. We've gotten more reports of Santas and baby Jesus's going missing. The Santas are all big, over three feet and the babies all have the manger attached. Nothing else is ever taken. And they are all from really old sets, at least forty years or more older, which makes it even worse as many of them were heirlooms."

"That's terrible. I hope you find them before Christmas. How many are missing? Santas that big, you'd need somewhere big to store them all."

"Twelve that I know of. It's possible some people haven't reported them. The thefts all seem to be confined to Appleby. How's the Holiday Tour going?"

"So far, so good. It's early though. We're testing the lights as we go, so we don't put up any dead lines. It's all just so time consuming and whoever had it before me, didn't leave any notes, so I'm figuring things out as I go along."

"Oh, that would have been Pete MacGregor. I'm surprised he didn't leave any notes behind. He was meticulous about everything."

"Funny, his son Alex gave me Pete's notes for the Fall Festival and there wasn't anything about the Holiday Tour in them. I'll give him a call and see if he remembers them. Why didn't any of the ladies tell me he ran it?"

Travis shrugged. "Maybe they didn't want to bring it up after his death."

I twisted my lips in thought. "That doesn't sound like the ladies I know. I'll ask them why they didn't say anything to me."

The atmosphere was great and I felt like a giddy school girl with a crush. Our chicken piccata and spaghetti arrived and smelled amazing. Steam rose from my plate making little swirls in the air. I couldn't wait to sink my teeth into it.

"You mentioned you're a big brother?" If a guy could glow, then Travis glowed as he began talking about becoming a big brother and the boys he was mentoring.

"The kids are just fantastic," he said when my phone buzzed. I silenced it and it buzzed again.

"Hold that thought," I said apologetically.

Shelby's frantic voice came over the line after I answered. It took me several minutes to calm her down enough to understand what she was saying. I grimaced at Travis after hanging up the phone. "Shelby is having family issues. I should probably go see her."

"You can't duck out on a friend in need," said Travis, but his eyes looked sad. "Neither one of us has started eating yet, why don't you take my food to Shelby and you two can eat together."

"Oh no, I couldn't do that. You need to eat too," I protested. I felt torn, Shelby really needed me but I really wanted to finish my dinner with Travis.

He put his hand on mine and I felt tingles go up my arm. "I insist. I'll just put in another order for myself. You go help your friend and we'll reschedule." He gave me one of his brilliant smiles that made my heart melt.

"Fine. But I insist on buying you lunch tomorrow."

"Agreed." He waved down the waitress and she packaged up our food. He walked me out to my car and we stood there awkwardly until he said, "next time I think I'll pick you up. And turn off your phone."

I gawked at him and then he winked at me and I laughed. "I will have the best lunch tomorrow. Thank you for being so understanding, Travis."

On a sudden impulse, I stretched up and gave him a quick peck on the cheek before ducking into my car. I felt as nervous as a school girl with a playground crush. As I pulled away, the illumination from my headlights gave me one last glance of his handsome face.

Shelby

"Oh my God, I don't know what to do," cried Shelby as she released me from a breath crushing hug. She was wearing rumpled sweats and her long brown hair was a tangled mess. "Dixie is letting her ex move back in and I know he's got a girl on the side. In fact he's got a son the same age as Grayson." I closed my eyes at the news and took a breath. Shelby had been all over the place emotionally for the past few months.

"You bring her over here and I'll have a talk with her," I said as I took the restaurant bag to the coffee table and made her sit down. Shelby and I had gone to school together and she was always a cup full of drama. I forced a fork and a container of food into her hands.

Shelby looked at the container bewildered. "How did you get food so fast?" she asked.

"I was out to dinner with Travis when you called," I replied.

Her eyes widened in shock. "Oh, Holly, I'm so sorry. I didn't mean to interrupt your date. Why didn't you say something?"

"It's not like you gave me a chance to talk." I took a bite of food and the chicken piccata just melted on my tongue. "Oh my, this food is delicious. You should eat. Travis was kind enough to give you his dinner. You owe me big time."

Over the remainder of the dinner, Shelby poured her heart out to me and I resolved to knock some philosophical common sense into her daughter.

"Look Shelbs, you can't control what your daughter does. She's going to have to make her own mistakes. Just let her know that you'll be there for her and I'll be there for you." I gave her a quick hug. "I'll talk to Dixie. Sometimes it helps when advice comes from a neutral third party."

"Thanks Holly."

"Now tell me what's really going on?" I said in my best mom voice.

Shelby shook her head. "What do you mean?"

"You've been a mess for weeks now and it's not your daughter."

Shelby's face crumpled. "They're forcing me to retire. They said I'm too old for undercover work."

"But you're only 58," I said indignantly.

Shelby fiddled with her hands in her lap. "They said I could move to a desk job." She looked up at me and tears glistened in her eyes. "I don't do desk jobs," she wailed.

I reached over and patted her hands. "Change is tough but it doesn't have to be bad. Is Scott retiring too?" Scott is her secret husband no one knows about but me.

"No. He wants an office job. He's been asking for it for years."

"I think you need to take it one step at a time. A desk job doesn't have to be boring. Maybe you could work in analysis. In the movies, it looks exciting."

She gave me a look I wasn't sure how to interpret. Either my comment was incredibly stupid or brilliant.

"Do you really think so?"

I handed her the box of tissues on the coffee table and she wiped her tears. "Okay. I'll give it a try."

I left the warmth of her house for the chill of the night air. The sky was clear and thousands of stars twinkled in the night sky. I crunched through the snow to my car and turned the heat on high. What a month this was turning out to be. It made me wonder what was going to happen next?

That Unsettled Feeling

Somehow I had managed to go several days without running into Bonnie which pleased me to no end but also made me nervous. What was she planning? She blamed me for Travis not donating his dead wife's face for her reconstruction after the car accident which she deliberately caused, and which resulted in the deaths of his wife and my husband. Of course, that's a whole other story. People can really be irrational. I probably should remember that as a life lesson.

Travis had been recalled to Morecroft so his investigation and our lunch was put on hold

I'd taken up karate classes with Mildred a few months ago so I could learn to defend myself after the incident when Carol Oates's neighbor Mike had tried to kill me and Gloria. It was actually kind of fun and relaxing. Mildred had been taking it for years and was a whiz at it. She claimed it was just for fun and a way to stay in shape, but her skills had actually come in handy a time or two.

The lights in the window spilled out onto the snow outside. Inside, I could see other students warming up in their Gi's. I welcomed the warmth of the gym as I entered and ducked into the locker room to change.

I scanned the room as I came out for Mildred. Despite it being five after the hour, she wasn't here yet. An uneasiness began to creep up my spine. She wanted to tell me something and now she wasn't here. I didn't even change my clothes, just grabbed my bag and left.

Driving past the candy shop, I could see it was all closed up and the lights were out. Just in case, I got out and checked the door. "Mildred? Are you here?" My calls went unanswered so I made the short 20 minute trip to her house, just down the street from mine. What could have happened to her? What did she want to talk about that she couldn't call me?

As I pulled up to her house, the windows were all lit up with lights. That's good right? I parked in the slush at the edge of the road and knocked on her door.

Her eyes lit up with relief when the door opened and she saw me, she hugged me and then pulled me into the living room. "Mildred I was worried when you weren't at karate." My voice trailed off as I took in the scene before me. Two women in their seventies with identical faces but opposite everything else, were seated on Mildred's small couch. One of them was dressed in a pantsuit and the other was in a dress. One had dark curly hair and the other had straight blonde hair.

Mildred indicated them with one hand. "Holly, I would like you to meet my twin sisters. They'll be staying here for a few days. This is my friend Holly. Be nice." I thought I heard my sweet Mildred scoff, 'as if,' under her breath.

"Holly have a seat. We ordered pizza, it should be here soon," said the twins in unison. I wandered over to the fireplace and sat on the chair next to it. "It's nice to meet you ladies."

"Likewise," said the curly brunette in the pantsuit. "I'm Dorothy, you can call me Dottie."

The chubby blonde in the dress with straight hair gave a smirk. "And you can call me Bettie."

"You mean Bertha," snickered Dottie.

Bettie glared at her. "I mean Bettie. I wouldn't have said it otherwise, Dorothy."

A ring from the doorbell interrupted this little spat. The twins looked at each other. "You get it," said Dottie.

Bettie settled herself deeper into the couch. "I think it's your turn. I distinctly remember having to turn off the lights at the house before we left. So it's definitely your turn."

"Yes. But at the airport, I'm the one who watched all the luggage while you used the restroom. For a very long time, I might add."

"I'll just get it," began Mildred when they both cut her off.

"No," they said together.

"Bettie is going to get it."

"It's already paid for," said Mildred. "We just have to open the door."

"Hey!" yelled a voice from outside. "I'm just going to set the pizza down out here. You might want to get it quick as it's pretty cold out. I think I see an ant."

Bettie gave Dottie a look and Dottie gave Bettie a look. At this point I was getting a little cold myself so I jumped to my feet without a word and opened the door. The pizza in all its pizza gloriousness was nestled on the cold porch step so I rescued it and took it inside to the kitchen where I promptly snagged a piece and ate it as I stared at the twins with an I dare you look.

Bettie stood up first, "I suppose we should eat it before it gets cold. Dottie can you grab some plates?"

"Stop telling me what to do," remarked Dottie. Mildred looked at me with a 'please help me' expression on her face. I grabbed a napkin and handed Mildred a piece of pizza. "Enjoy it while you can," I whispered.

The twins retired to the couch to eat in comfort. "You've got to help me," whispered Mildred back.

"Are they always like this?"

"Yes. My entire life and they pounce on me if I try to keep the peace. If you hadn't opened the door, that pizza probably would have frozen out there."

"I hear you. You're welcome to stay at my place until they leave," I offered.

Mildred's eyes lit up. "Really?"

"Absolutely." I walked back into the living room. "Ladies. Mildred's house is so small that we really feel you should have it to yourselves. She's grabbing a suitcase and will be staying with me. That way, you each get your own room and will be more comfortable."

Mildred had run into her bedroom when I started talking and was now back with a duffle bag with various clothing items sticking out of the top.

"Okay, girls, it's been lovely to see you. If you need anything, I'm just a couple houses up at Holly's. Text if you need anything. C'mon Holly. Bye!"

We were out the door and it shut behind us before the twins had a chance to respond. She grabbed my car door, jumped inside and locked it behind her like a demon was chasing her. "Hurry Holly, before they come out."

I put the car in gear and pulled away from the curb. "It's going to take them at least twenty minutes of arguing to decide who's going to open the front door. I don't think you have to worry." I reached over and patted her on the knee. "Is this what you were trying to tell me?"

Mildred sighed. "Yes but I couldn't decide if it was really important or just annoying to me. I wanted to know if you thought I could get away with putting them in a hotel but I figured they would just hunt me down. Where are we going?"

"Hm, well, I noticed you didn't tell them where my house is so I thought we could take the long way around and then they won't see us pulling into the driveway."

"Oh, you are so smart. That's why I like you Holly."

Thirty minutes later, we were snuggled on the couch in our pjs with cups of hot chocolate, by candlelight because she had insisted on turning off the lights and pulling the curtains closed just in case. I had to let Mildred borrow a nightgown because she had somehow ended up with three pairs of pants, one blouse, two pairs of underwear, three socks and one bra. She said she would go shopping tomorrow.

"I hear Travis is investigating the Christmas decoration thefts. Has he had any luck?" she asked.

"I don't think so. Captain Moran sent him back to Morecroft. Here's another weird thing I was thinking of discussing with the book club," I said, changing the subject. We had started a book club with a very select group of women that was really cover for a murder mystery group.

"The woman who bought Carol Oates's house called me because someone dug a hole in her backyard. A body shaped hole that was four feet deep." I looked at her for her opinion. When she didn't answer I continued.

"It had red flakes in it. Do you think there could have been a Santa Claus buried there?"

"That is pretty peculiar."

"Right? And Jacob Martin that lives around the corner wanted to buy Carol's house and was angry when he found out it was sold. Could he have dug it up?

Mildred was quiet for a long time staring at her hands folded in her lap. "I've lived here for quite a long time and it seems to me I recall some of the old timers talking about a secret. I asked my husband about it and he feigned ignorance of the whole thing but I'm sure it was something to do with the Blume House." She looked up and shrugged. "Like I said it was a long time ago, shortly after that, they quit having Christmas at the house."

"That is interesting. What connection could these thefts have with the past? I told Gloria to check into letting the city let us use the house for the Christmas Tour this year. I should check in and see what she found out."

I yawned and then Mildred yawned followed by Ginger and Friendly. "I suppose we should be getting to bed, there's no telling what trouble my sisters will get up to tomorrow."

Who Killed Santa?

I was awoken the next morning by my phone jangling. Hoping it wasn't the twins, I groaned and rolled over to grab my phone off the nightstand. I vaguely recalled being chased by Santa and having to dodge baby Jesus's in my dreams last night leaving me tired this morning.

"Hello?" I mumbled into the receiver.

"Mom? You've got to get over here right now." My daughter Penelope's voice sounded frightened and angry over the phone line.

"Penelope? What's going on and where's here?" I swung my legs over the side of the bed and sat up, listening with concern.

"I went by my storage to get my Christmas decorations out and the unit next to me is just filled with destroyed decorations. Chloe said you were looking into the missing Christmas decorations."

"Text me the address and I'll be right there," I said. I disconnected the call and crossed to my closet where I pulled out some jeans and a sweater. Then I remembered Mildred.

Calling Ginger and Friendly I headed to the kitchen intending to start a pot of coffee and found Mildred already had it going along with toast and eggs.

"I get up really early," she said in explanation. "Are you headed out? Could you drop me off at the Candy Shop?"

"Thanks Mildred, that's really kind of you. My daughter called, I've got to run to her storage unit. It might be a clue to the Christmas thefts. I don't suppose you can make that breakfast to go?"

With the animals taken care of and breakfast in hand, Mildred and I hopped in the car for the short ride into town. The storage units were at the near end of town so Mildred decided to stop at the storage facility with me.

Chloe looked like her little heart was going to break as I surveyed the devastation with dismay. Shattered pieces of plastic Santa were scattered everywhere throughout the room. Chloe let out a short piercing scream. "Nana! Who killed Santa?" She was only four and Santa was very real to her.

"It's okay, sweetheart. It's not really Santa, just the plastic one that goes on the roof."

"I know but he might think we did it and put us on the naughty list and not bring us any presents," she sobbed.

I gave her a comforting hug. "Santa knows you're a good girl honey. And he knows who is on the naughty list too. He's magical. So you don't have to worry, okay?"

Chloe looked up at me with her beautiful blue eyes opened wide. "Are you sure Nana?" I wiped the tears off her cheeks. "I'm positive honey."

"Okay, then let's catch the bad people." Smiling at her positive attitude, I gave her another hug and then called Travis who promised to be there shortly.

"Honey," I said to my daughter. "Why don't you and Chloe get your Christmas decorations and go home. I can wait for Travis. Would you mind dropping Mildred off at her store?"

"Sure, mom."

While she and Chloe retrieved the decorations, Mildred and I looked over the scene more closely. "What do you think Holly?"

"It certainly looks like Santas were destroyed here, but I don't see any baby Jesus's."

"Maybe the culprit still has an ounce of sense left in their head," said Mildred. "Bad enough destroying Santa, I guess they couldn't bring themselves to break baby Jesus."

I knelt and picked up a piece of plastic, the red coating looked new and shiny. How do you even break a plastic Santa in this many pieces?

Penelope finished and collected Mildred and left. Travis showed up about 15 minutes later.

"What do you think?" I asked. "Does it seem to be related to your thefts?" He walked around and surveyed the damage. There seems to be more damage here than the number of thefts that have been reported. It's weird that the storage door is open. It's almost as if someone wanted us to find it."

"To get you to stop looking?" I asked.

He stood there with his arms crossed, tapping his right forefinger against his lips. "I think I should go talk to the person in the office here and see who this unit is registered to."

In the cramped office a man in his early twenties was kicking back in his chair with his feet up, watching a basketball game on his phone and munching on chips. He had a physique that looked like he enjoyed too many of them. He glanced up as we entered. "Can I help you?"

"Hi, I'm Detective Travis Smart with the Appleby police department. Could you tell me who is renting unit 19?"

He sat up and leaned over the computer. "I can't tell you who is renting it but I can let you know if it is rented." He punched the buttons on the keyboard. "Nope, that unit is vacant. Why do you want to know?"

"It's filled with broken Santa's."

"Say what now?" He scratched his head.

"Maybe you should come take a look," suggested Travis. Moments later, the three of us were back in front of unit 19.

"Uh, that shouldn't be there. It's been vacant for a month."

"Do you lock the vacant units?" asked Travis, looking at his name badge, "Sean."

"Nah, we don't usually have issues with people storing stuff in unused units."

"Sean, when's the last time you checked this unit?" I asked.

"We don't. Not until someone is going to rent it. Like I said, we don't usually have any issues with the empty units, unless you count dust and spiders."

"What about security cameras?"

The man grimaced. "The storage drive broke a couple months ago. Haven't had the money to fix it. Like I said,"

"I know, I know," said Travis. "You don't usually have problems. Thanks for your time, Sean. If you find anything that could be of use to me, give me a call." He handed Sean his business card and we left.

"That didn't go well," I said as we walked back to our vehicles. "Any update on Laurie Culpepper's death?"

Travis stopped and I had to turn to look back at him. "What about Laurie's death? She slipped and fell," he said slowly. "Don't tell me you're looking into an accidental death?"

I put on my best innocent look. "Okay, I won't."

He sighed and shook his head. "Why don't I believe you?"

"The ladies are upset about her accident and asked me to take a look but I have to agree with you, it looks like it was an accidental death. Except."

"Except, what?"

"She died in the middle of the day and no one noticed her? Nobody was walking their dog by or getting their mail? How long was she there after she died?"

"Holly, you know I can't tell you that."

I bit my bottom lip. "Did you notice the treeline goes right to the sidewalk where she was found? And the girls swear Laurie hated the snow. She would never be caught going for a walk in it if she didn't have to."

"None of that is evidence of foul play."

"I agree, but I promised the girls to take a look. What could it hurt?"

"Okay. But stay out of trouble."

"Of course," I smiled at him. "What trouble could I possibly get into?"

The rest of the day was uneventful. I cleared up my work at the office and picked up Mildred from the candy store. By unspoken consent, we were carpooling together. Neither of us wanted to run into the twins if we didn't have to.

Mildred and I were just sitting down to dinner when there was a knock at the door. Ginger ran to the window and began wagging her tail vigorously. At least that meant there was someone friendly at the door.

I opened it prepared to cheerfully greet whoever it was when my mouth fell open.

I hadn't seen the short stocky woman in the stylish grey coat standing there in over a year.

"Mom?"

She reached in and gave me a big hug. "Holly! I've come to spend Christmas with you! Isn't that exciting?"

It was a good thing she was hugging me and couldn't see the look of dismay on my face. My mother was a class A narcissist and saw no problems in taking over my life and telling me how wrong I was. For the last several years, she had been living with my sister and making her life miserable. I extricated myself from her embrace and took several steps back.

"Is everything okay with Donna?" I asked concerned. What could possibly have possessed my mother to leave sunny Florida for the snow covered mountains?

My mom tossed her head and rolled her eyes at the same time, making me think she was about to have a stroke. "Nonsense. Donna is fine. Does there have to be something wrong for me to want to come see my darling daughter?"

Um pretty much. I would definitely have to call my sister and find out what the heck was going on.

"Who is this absolutely ravishing lady here? Aren't you going to introduce us?"

"Sorry, this is my friend Mildred, she's currently staying with me." I emphasized the staying with me part. "Mildred, this is my mom, Lily Devine"

Mildred was looking a little worried until I said the staying with me part. She reached out to shake my mom's hand but was instead enveloped in a hug. "Any friend of Holly's is family to me," she smiled at both of us. "Where should I put my stuff?"

"I can call and get you a reservation at the hotel across town. We can drop you off after dinner. I'm sure you would be much more comfortable there than on the couch."

"A hotel?" she looked horrified.

"Mom. I don't have room here. This place only has two bedrooms. If you would have just called and let me know you were coming…"

"Since when do I have to have reservations to stay at my daughter's house? I'll just take your room."

"You'll do no such thing. I have a job and I need my sleep. The hotel is only half an hour away. You'll be fine. They have a lovely restaurant right downstairs and you'll have a great view of the mountains and lake. Plus all the skiers are there right now, I'm sure there's plenty of single men there as well."

She looked about to argue until I mentioned the men, which is exactly why I mentioned the men. What were the chances that Mildred and I would both end up with unwanted guests this Christmas?

My mom huffed. "Since I have to go to the hotel, I may as well eat there. Make your call."

She flounced over to the couch. "This couch smells like dog. Don't you ever clean it for heaven's sake? I will expect you to pick me up for lunch tomorrow. Do you think you can manage that? I haven't seen you in over a year. Oh, and bring my great granddaughter with you."

I stepped into my bedroom to make the call and promised the desk clerk an extra fifty dollars to make this work. After some shuffling around, he let me know they'd found a room for her. Folding my hands and looking up to the ceiling, I mouthed the words, "thank you God."

Mom

My mom had a bad habit of walking in unannounced when I was a child, so I had taken to locking the bedroom door when I was changing. With her back in town, I found myself automatically doing it again even though she was staying at the hotel. Trauma I guess. It wasn't even 6 a.m. when I was awoken by her banging on my bedroom door. "Holly, do you have a boy in there?"

"A boy mom? Seriously, how old do you think I am?" I pulled my robe off the hook on the back of the bathroom door and wrapped it around myself as I opened the door.

"What took you so long? Did he go out the window?" She ran to look through the curtains as I just sighed and entered the kitchen. I didn't even bother with the coffee machine which I had preset the night before. Although the smell of the coffee was enticing, I had something I needed to do first.

"Holly, you're not entertaining *men* in your room at night are you?"

Instead of answering, I opened the back door. "Mom, why don't you go take a look? It snowed last night. I'm sure you can find some footprints."

My mom sniffed and tossed her head as she headed out the door. After she passed through, I shut and locked it. Mildred observed the action from her position by the stove where bacon sat sizzling in a pan.

I sat on the couch enjoying my coffee as I ignored the furious knocking on the backdoor. Mildred looked at me. "Aren't you going to let her in?"

"Nah, she lives for this stuff."

Mildred continued to stare at me. "It's pretty cold out there."

Friendly hopped into my lap and I scratched her furry little chin. "Don't worry, I'll let her in in a minute. She does go on so, about learning lessons. Do you think she'll learn from this lesson?" Her black button eyes looked into mine, like she was staring into the depths of my soul. "Nope, I don't think so either."

Reluctantly, I got to my feet and opened the back door. "Did you find what you were looking for?" I asked innocently.

She squished her face up and glared at me. "You know very well I did not."

"You should probably come inside, it's pretty cold out there. I just made a pot of coffee," I said, ignoring her comment. Shelby thought she had problems. Dixie's got nothing on my mom.

"Holly," she began in a sweet voice. "You know I'm just looking out for you. Men aren't going to marry you if they can get what they want for free."

"Well, mom, first I'd have to actually have a man in my life. Although I suppose I could pay one of them to sleep with me. I might have to go to Morecroft to find one though." I tapped my finger against my lips thoughtfully.

My mom spun around with her hands on her hips. "Holly Ann Holcraft, you will do no such thing. No daughter of mine is paying for...for."

"Sex, mom. The word is sex. I'm just kidding. Lighten up or you'll have a heart attack."

Cue the pouting. "Holly dear, I just want what's best for you. It's been ten years, you need to move on with your life. Perhaps, I can find a nice man for you."

"Okay, mom, just stop. I'm perfectly happy with my life right now and I don't need a man to make me feel better. I'm going to shower now or I'll be late for work. There's food in the fridge and Katie May's in town makes an awesome breakfast." Too late, I remembered it was right next to my office. I might need to enlist the help of the book club ladies if I was going to survive her visit. I wonder if Travis would be the one arresting me for her murder?

The thought of Travis gave me pleasant thoughts that carried me through my shower and dressing. I re-entered the kitchen to find my mom had taken over making breakfast from Mildred. "That smells delicious but I've really got to get to work."

"I knew you would say that," she said smugly. "That's why I made you breakfast sandwiches and lunch to take with you." She handed me a huge paper bag.

"Uh, thanks, mom but I thought I was meeting you for lunch?"

"I've got other plans. We'll do it another time."

"Don't feed Ginger and Friendly too much. I don't need them getting upset stomachs." I'm sure Joe will help me eat the lunch. Ginger gave me the sad eye and Friendly jumped on the counter and meowed at me. Mom was even turning my own animals against me.

"You named your cat Friendly?"

"Actually, she picked the name."

She waved the spatula in the air with one hand on her hip. Inwardly I sighed. "Holly you cannot seriously be yelling out the door calling 'Friendly'."

My mouth formed an 'o' and then I sucked my lips in. I had never thought about that. Was it too late to change her name?

"Hmph," she said and turned back to the stove to flip over a pancake in the shape of Mickey Mouse. "You'd better get going before you're late."

I waited until we were in the car and pulling away from the house to speak to Mildred but she spoke up first.

"I'm sorry Holly. I tried to stop her. I really did."

"It's okay Mildred. My mom is a force of nature to deal with once she gets going. How are your sisters getting along?"

"I've been afraid to ask."

"They haven't called. That's a good sign right?"

Mildred gave the deepest, saddest sigh I have ever heard. "Holly, how am I going to get them out of my house?"

"We could introduce them to my mom. Maybe they will keep each other entertained."

Mildred grimaced at the thought. She looked just like that emoji that shows all it's teeth. I didn't realize people actually made those faces.

Changing the subject, I said, "Mildred, how come no one told me Pete used to run the Holiday Tours?"

"No one told you?" she asked shocked.

"No," I said shaking my head.

"I assumed someone did. Didn't Alex give you his notes?"

"No notes. Did he leave notes?"

"Why yes, he had detailed notes of everything. I'm surprised Alex didn't have them."

"Well, the house is sold now and everything is gone."

"Didn't you tell us that someone broke into his house after he died? Maybe they stole them."

I looked at her in shock. "Why on earth would anyone steal notes about a charity function?"

"Watch the road!" she yelled sharply. I looked up to see I was drifting into the other lane.

"Really, I might as well be driving with Gloria," she said snippily.

"I'm calling a meeting of the book club for tonight. We need to find out if anyone found out anything about Laurie and I have some questions to ask about the Holiday Tour and the Christmas thefts."

"I'll make the calls," said Mildred. "Does six o'clock work for you?"

"Yes. We may have to do it by candlelight and I'll hide my car in the garage."

"Sounds good. Maybe I'll suggest the movie theater to my sisters. A text should do it," she added.

Fatigue

Shortly after reaching the office, I was called up by Patty and then Cindy and then other volunteers and I found myself running all over town solving problems. By noon I was exhausted. It's one thing to manage an event that's in one location, as the Fall Festival had been, this was entirely different. We had twelve houses on the list scattered all over town and it was constant traveling from one location to the next. I'd had to shove my real estate work off on Joe.

The plan had been to have all the decorations out and ready to go at each house and my group of volunteers would do one house a day up until the day of the event.

But you know what they say about the best laid plans. Mice had chewed through several of the light cords, ornaments got broken. Some decorations were put away in boxes without lids and were more than dusty. Trips had to be made for replacements and of course, we couldn't put up broken lights, so now our days were spent traveling from one location to another and piecemealing things together. It's not like anyone could really be blamed, the Tour of Holiday Homes had been going on for fourteen years and decorations had just fallen into disarray. My biggest job at this point was to keep repeating, "it's okay, once the lights are up, it will all fall into place," over and over again.

Volunteers had started nodding their heads each time I said it and saying, "we know, we know." But you know what? It's okay. Next year will go much more smoothly. Wait. Am I doing this again next year? What am I thinking?

Emmeline was beaming as she opened her door to me. She had decorated her house as the Nightmare before Christmas. I think it was an attempt to get back at Alma who loves the holiday season more than any other. At least this was one house that was finished and there were no Santas to steal here which got me thinking.

"Emmeline, your house is absolutely wonderful. You've done a great job and finished early."

"Thanks Holly, I love decorating." She spun in a circle as we took all the decorations in. Jack Skellington was on the lawn with his dog dressed as a reindeer. Other characters were putting decorations on shrubbery.

"How's Alma taking it?"

"Weelp, she's not overly enthusiastic about it," she said, "but she admitted it came together nicely."

"That was gracious of her. Where's Albert? Is he coming for Christmas too?"

"Alma said he'll be here for Christmas day."

"How do you feel about that?" I asked. Alma had sold the house to Emmeline on the condition she gets one last Christmas in it.

"It's okay. I like her and Albert is really nice and it's just this one time. I think," she added as an afterthought.

I laughed. "She certainly seems to be involved in town business for someone who's moving to Florida. Is she here?"

"Nope, went to the store, I think. Did you need her?"

"I just wanted to pick her brains. It's okay, I'm sure I'll run into her." Emmeline gave me the grand tour of the house. It was so nice to see this event bringing her out of her shell. As we got back to the living room the door opened and Alma walked in.

"Holly, it's so good to see you. How's the Holiday Tour coming along?"

I smiled brightly at her. "It's coming together. I was wondering if you had Pete's notes from the previous Tours?"

"Notes? They should have been given to you when you took over." she looked concerned.

"Nope, nobody gave me anything. In fact, I didn't even know Pete used to be in charge."

"Oh Holly, that's terrible, I'm sorry, but you seem to be doing well and everything is coming along nicely."

"Yes, and Gloria is looking into using the Blume house for an additional Christmas display."

Alma wrinkled her brow. "The Blume house? Why would you want to use that?"

Something about her words struck me as odd and I watched her reaction closely. "Gloria remembered how it used to be decorated so beautifully for Christmas and suggested we do it again. I put her in charge of it."

"Didn't you say we already had a dozen homes? I don't really think we need another one do you?"

Shrugging my shoulders, I said, "Gloria got a bug about it, so I figured what would it hurt to let her try. It looked fantastic for the Fall Festival."

"Yes it did." She smiled politely, "I guess it's for the city to decide. If you'll excuse me, I've got some calls to make, last minute Christmas gifts you know."

Emmeline waited until she left the room to speak. "She's hiding something."

I looked at her curiously. "What?"

"She's hiding something. I know her and something about using the Blume house is bothering her. I bet she's going to call the mayor."

I looked at her, at a loss for words. "I should go too. If you hear anything let me know and again, your house looks fantastic. Thanks for getting it done so quickly."

That took a weird turn. I walked back to my car and found a note on the windshield. I unfolded it and my heart began beating fast. "Stop this investigation or else." I looked around but here was no one in sight. It was broad daylight and the snow around my car was trampled down so I would never be able to find footprints. Why would someone care about missing Christmas decorations?

A lot of nothing

When I got back to the office exhausted, my mom was waiting for me outside the office door.

"Mom, I thought you had plans?"

"I just wanted to see where my sweetheart works. Where is my great granddaughter?" she added with a pout.

"She has gymnastics class and again, you said you had plans." Inwardly, I sighed. There was so much work to do and the last thing I needed was my mom hanging around asking questions.

"Hi Holly, who's this charming lady?" The sudden voice behind me made me jump.

"Travis you scared me. This is my mom. Mom, this is Travis. He's investigating the Christmas ornament thefts." As I introduced him, my Mom instantly transformed into Mrs. Seductiveness.

"Oh, my, aren't you handsome." She stretched out her hand. "I'm Holly's mom, Lily Devine. Travis's eyebrows rose as he glanced at me.

"So nice to meet you Lily," he said. "Are you staying for the holidays?" Clearly he had a lot to learn about my mother. You never give her an opening.

With a grin that would have made the Grinch proud, she said, "Yes I am. Are you going to be around for the holidays? Perhaps you could show me the town? I'm so excited about Holly's little Christmas festival. It's time she expanded her horizons."

Travis opened his mouth to speak but no words came out. In fact, he looked a little bewildered.

"Mom. Don't be silly. Travis is a police detective and he's going to be busy, too busy to show you around. Come on, I want to introduce you to some friends of mine." I grabbed her elbow before she had a chance to say anything more and hustled her down the street to Mildred's candy shop hoping someone I knew was there. As I glanced back at Travis he looked relieved and mouthed 'thank you' to me.

Fortunately, I discovered there were three ladies inside that I did know after we pushed through the door, making the little bell over it tinkle. "Mom, I'd like you to meet Gloria, Cindy and Maggs. They're really close friends of mine and they've lived here for years. ladies, I have work to do would you mind showing my mom around town?"

My mom's expression flickered between a polite smile and dismay. Inside I was high-fiving myself. Between the four ladies, my mom would be too exhausted to care what I was doing.

They made her sit down at the table with them and she gave me a pleading look that I pretended not to notice.

Gloria squinted her eyes as she contemplated why I was making the request. "Sure Holly, not a problem," she finally said. She winked at me and I knew I was going to pay for this favor later.

"Lily, you've got to tell me all about your visit. How do you like Appleby?"asked Cindy. Before my mom realized what was happening, she was whisked out the door.

I hurried out the door before anyone could change their minds. Back at my desk, I had to know what was so interesting about Carol's old property, so I did a title search on it. Carol had owned it for three years before selling it and moving away.

Prior to that, it had been owned by a Phillip Harding for over 30 years but was transferred into a trust ten years ago. This wasn't unusual as people did this all the time to avoid probate. The name didn't ring a bell so I did an internet search for the name.

There was a Phillip Harding in Delaware that was a doctor, a twenty something on Facebook, three college students, and a painter. None of them really seemed to fit. maybe Lucy or Vana would be able to find the information or, I just might need to visit the library and look it up on the microfiche.

I have gave them each a quick text and then focused my attention on my clients. Tom Franks's escrow was proceeding quickly and would close before the holidays were over. It was wonderful how having a new grandchild could change his heart.

My search for homes for a new buyer was interrupted by a ding from my phone. Lucy had found the address for Phillip Harding.

Sometimes I didn't know how she did it. He now lived in Florida. It was still early enough so I took a chance and gave him a call.

"Hello?"

"Mr. Harding? Phillip Harding?"

"Yes, this is me."

"Hi, my name is Holly Holcraft. I'm a real estate agent in Appleby. I understand you used to own some property out here?"

"Yes. It was sold years ago."

"Yes, well, the new owner recently contacted me and I was wondering if you had ever buried anything in the backyard? Like a time capsule or something?"

There was a moment of silence on the other end. "Mr. Harding are you still there?"

"Yes. Why? Did somebody find something?"

"No, unless you count an empty hole and some paint flakes something. I was just wondering if you knew anything about it?"

This time there was a longer silence but I waited it out.

"Not that I can recall. I can't imagine what the red flakes are from," he finally replied. "Well, if you do find out what it was, would you let me know?"

"Of course, Mr. Harding." I disconnected the call. That was another dead end. Maybe one of the ladies in the book club would have a clue.

Book Club

Everyone arrived at my house promptly at six pm. Mildred ran through lighting candles and shutting off all the lights, while the other ladies just looked confused.

"Are we having a seance?" Cindy finally asked.

"Mildred, do you want to explain or shall I?" I asked. Mildred dropped to the couch. "I don't suppose you would believe I was just setting the mood?" Glancing around the room, she looked down at her clasped hands in her lap. "I didn't think so. Please don't judge me too harshly. My twin sisters are in town and they are absolutely unbearable. They fight nonstop all day long so I've been avoiding them."

"You can't hide from them forever," I said. "Although, the timing was extremely fortuitous for me. Ladies, how did you manage to ditch my mom?"

"Oh, that was easy," said Maggs. "We introduced her to a nice gentleman at the hotel. She'll be busy for a while."

"Because you paid him to take her to dinner," exclaimed Cindy.

"It was Gloria's idea," retorted Maggs. "Don't put it all on me."

Gloria twirled her red hair on her finger. "I just know what women like her want. Besides, he owed me a favor."

It was definitely time to change the subject. "Now to get down to business, Gloria, what did you find out about using the Blume house for Christmas?"

Gloria cocked her head to the side and smiled. She really was quite attractive. "I managed to get Mayor Townsend to give me permission to use it. He's up for reelection next year you know and he really liked all the publicity from the Fall Festival. The positive publicity," she corrected. Apparently, that meant not the bear or the dead body that showed up. "Plus, I used my girlish charms to sway him to my side."

"Great, I don't need to know what charms you used," I said quickly. "Okay, any update on Laurie's death?" I glanced at each of the ladies in turn.

Maggs spoke up first. "The coroner said he couldn't pinpoint a firm time as she was frozen but it had to have happened prior to 3 pm because she was already stiff and it would have taken a while for her body to freeze."

"So she did die before that time. Was there any blood on the sidewalk when she hit her head? Anything to suggest that perhaps she had been moved?" I looked from blank face to blank face.

Cindy, with her short, blonde curls framing her innocent face, glanced at Maggs before speaking. "I, we, didn't think to ask that question. We'll go back."

I sighed. "Ladies, when investigating a possible death, we need to consider all the angles. If she fell on the sidewalk, there possibly could have been blood left behind if she hit it hard enough. If there was a head wound and there is no blood, that would indicate the body was moved. If there is no head wound, then we just don't know either way. The only way to find out, is to ask questions."

"How do we know what we should ask, if we don't know?" inquired Maggs.

"Lesson one," I said, even though I wasn't a professional investigator but I am a good real estate agent and asking questions is vital. "Look at the scene analytically. What would you expect to find if it was a murder? What would you expect to find if it wasn't? Then ask questions to confirm your suspicions. The best questions are ones you already know the answer to."

Cindy raised her hand before speaking. I'd given up on telling her it wasn't necessary. "How do we know the answers?"

"You are surmising the answers? The questions confirm them."

"Surmise?" Frowned Cindy.

"Are there any other questions we should ask?" interrupted Maggs. You'll never catch her raising her hand.

I clasped my hands together out of frustration, crushing my fingers between the joints, my knuckles turning white. "Ladies, you need to think about the situation and ask questions, throw out ideas. This book club isn't going to work if you all expect me to solve everything. We're a team. If we were discussing a book what would you ask?"

Mildred popped up. "But we would have the facts from the book to help us."

Cindy sat up straight like a light bulb had gone on. "But we do have facts," she said excitedly. "We know when she died and where and what she was wearing. Isn't that right Holly?"

"Now you're getting it. Take what you know and question it. Were her clothes warm enough? Remember Pete wasn't wearing appropriate clothing. What do we know about Laurie?"

Maggs and Mildred both shook their heads and said, "she hated the cold" together then looked at each other in surprise.

"Jinx!" yelled Maggs. "You owe me a coffee."

"But it's supposed to be a coke," complained Mildred.

Maggs tossed her head. "I don't like coke and I do like coffee."

"Ladies! Can we get back to the problem?" I asked, intervening before the argument got out of hand.

"Fine, coffee it is, which reminds me, I need to take a dress over for Laurie to be buried in," said Mildred sadly.

"Oh, she looked beautiful in the blue gown from the Christmas party.

You should take that one," exclaimed Cindy. "I think she would like that. She bought it specially for the party."

"You don't think it's too much, do you?" ask Mildred.

"Oh, no. I saw the pictures," commented Maggs. "She should look lovely when they bury her."

Something in my brain was bugging me during this conversation but every time I thought about it, it wriggled away like a wet bar of soap. "It will be lovely," I said. "Now on to another problem. What have you heard about the recent Christmas thefts?"

The four ladies glanced at each other. "Gloria?" questioned Cindy.

Gloria grimaced. "They've been happening all over town. Everyone's Santa over three feet tall has disappeared from their sets. Poor lonely reindeer are everywhere."

"Don't forget the baby Jesus's from the nativity sets," piped up Cindy. The ladies all shook their heads sadly.

"It's preposterous," retorted Maggs. "Who in their right mind would steal during Christmas? It's a sacrilege, I tell you."

"Are there any clues? Any evidence left behind?" I asked.

"Oh, that's a good question," said Cindy.

"You forgot to raise your hand," said Maggs. Cindy looked shocked and put her hand to her face.

"Maggs! Cindy, I told you, you don't need to raise your hand."

Mildred pursed her lips and looked innocently at her nails on her right hand. "Haven't you spoken with Travis about this?"

I rolled my eyes. "I have been in contact with him but not in the last couple days. We've been busy.

"Two little love birds sitting in a tree, k.i.s.s…" began Maggs.

"Maggs!" I cautioned. "Back to the subject. Any clues?" I asked again.

"Nothing has been mentioned by any of the victims," stated Mildred with a glare at Maggs.

"Gloria," I said, interrupting her mugging that had been directed toward Maggs. I swear these women are like little children. Gloria sat up straighter and looked at me expectantly. "Gloria, what can you tell me about the Christmas holidays at the Blume house?" There was something about Alma's comment about the holidays there that bothered me.

"Oh, they were so wonderful. There was a giant nativity scene that was set up on the lawn every year. People in town complained about it, the anti-church people, so the mayor had a Santa and reindeer display set up next to it. Oh, you should have heard the complaints. It was discontinued in the eighties, I don't know why."

Her eyes had lit up at the memory and then her face fell as she recalled the end of the celebration.

"Did you live here then?" asked Cindy quietly.

"Oh, no. My parents brought me. People used to come from all the neighboring towns to see it. That's why I want to bring it back, so other kids can have good memories."

"That's so nice," said Mildred.

"Mildred, did you see the nativity?" I asked.

"Oh, no. That was before we moved here. Way, before," she said.

"Maggs, Cindy, what about you?" They both shook their heads.

"Why don't you ladies ask around and see if anyone else in town remembers the holiday? Maybe we could do it the same way?" I suggested.

Gloria clapped her hands. "Oh, that would be wonderful," she smiled.

"On a side note," said Cindy as she put her hand in the air to get my attention. "I know Travis is looking into the recent thefts and I saw an advertisement for used Christmas decorations for sale. You don't suppose someone is stealing them to resell them, do you?"

"That's a brilliant idea," I said, and grabbed my phone to look up 'decorations for sale'. The other ladies did the same and silence reigned for all of two minutes.

"Oh, look here," exclaimed Cindy. *"Christmas decorations for sale, Santas, nativities, Christmas ornaments, garland, too much to mention. First come, first served. 1224 Limbeck Lane, Morecroft.*

"That's sounds promising," I said. "Let's go check it out first thing tomorrow."

"Tomorrow morning?" questioned Maggs. "I was going to go to the store."

"You can drive your own car and leave after we look."

"But I'll need to get gas..." She cut off as she saw my warning look. She had learned during the Fall Festival that I wasn't going to put up with her nonsense. "Fine, I'll just go later."

"I thought so. I'll drive. You ladies keep looking in case there's another sale close by." Maggs opened her mouth to speak and Cindy whapped her on the shoulder. Cindy might look innocent, but she's got a mean streak.

Junk

The address in Morecroft turned out to be a small thrift store business. I parked at the curb in front and we all peered at the window filled with, how shall I put this nicely? Junk. Just random items that bore no similarity. Most storefronts have some sort of theme to them but this one was filled with every holiday mixed up together.

There were so many items all jumbled together, you could look at it for an hour and still not see everything.

"I guess we should go in," whispered Mildred without opening her door.

Gloria let out a whoosh of air from her lips and pulled the latch to the door. "Might as well get it over with. How bad could it be inside?" We all turned to look at her but she was already ducking out the car door.

Inside, was no better or worse than the front display. Actually, I don't think it was a display, just junk thrown together.

"Hello." A plump woman with a beaming smile greeted us from behind a bare counter containing only a cash register. It was the only bare spot in the entire store. "Welcome to Agatha's Aggregations. Let me know if you need help finding anything." The other women glanced around without moving from their spot in front of the door. Tiny paths were cleared through the ceiling high shelves which were filled with every bric-a-brac you could think of.

"Thank you Agatha. I'm Holly and I'm a…" I cut off because I wasn't here as a real estate agent. Old habits are hard to break. "We," I said, indicating all of us with my hand. "Are here looking for a Santa to go with our Christmas display. Your ad said you had Santas?"

"Mmm, yes," said Agatha. "But I'm not Agatha. I'm Wendy Curran, there isn't actually an Agatha, I just liked the name." She smiled again as she lifted her shoulders in a shrug.

I glanced around, not seeing any Santas.

Wendy noticed our glances. "Sorry for the abundance of merchandise, I just find it so hard to say no to re-homing neglected items." Our eyebrows rose during her speech.

I nodded sympathetically. It's best to empathize with people rather than judge their motives. "Of course. Where do you get all this?" I asked waving my hand around to indicate the entire space.

Wendy's eyes lit up. "Oh, well, my husband and I, we buy the contents from old storage units that have gone unpaid." Maggs pursed her lips at this information and Wendy hurried on. "It's usually ones that people forget about or someone died and there are no relatives. Sometimes it is people who can't make the payments, but that's not that frequent out here."

"Have you ever found anything really valuable?" asked an excited Gloria. I could see her mind calculating the possibilities.

Wendy pursed her lips and shook her head no. "I always hold out the possibility but not really. You'd be surprised how many people like to buy these old ornaments though. They've become very popular over the years. I think part of it is the nostalgia of that time. I picked up a new lot just this week from an estate sale. Come see."

She motioned with her hand excitedly for us to follow her.

So we did. The back of the store was unlike the front. Rows of boxes were laid out evenly and each one was labeled. My eyebrows rose at the incongruity of it all. We didn't stop at the back of the store though, we continued on and out the back and across a small gravel lot to a house behind it. Wendy punched in numbers on the keypad and the garage door rose to reveal the biggest mess I had ever seen. Front and foremost though, was a four foot Santa that had seen better days. The plastic was so faded it was nearly impossible to make out the original colors.

"Put some paint on this baby, and he'll look great on a roof or in the front yard," said Wendy, putting her hand on Santa's shoulder like it was an old friend.

"We'll take it. How much?" I asked, the words tumbling out of my mouth before I had a chance to think. Four pairs of eyes looked at me in surprise and one pair in eager anticipation.

"I could let it go for hmm, fifty bucks," declared Wendy.

Maggs pushed her way to the front of Santa and looked Wendy in the eyes. "He's old, faded, and there are no reindeer to accompany him. He's just a lonely old man that needs work, like so many of us nowadays. We'll give you twenty-five dollars and guarantee him a comfortable life. Final offer."

Wendy met Maggs stare for stare. She squinted her eyes and tilted her head, still maintaining eye contact. After thirty seconds, she stuck out her hand. You've got a deal."

Money passed hands and the ladies carried Santa like a coffin around the side of the building. There was just no way, he was going to fit through the aisles in the store. Wendy closed the garage door and we walked back through the store to the entrance. I couldn't help it, the real estate agent in me just burst out thinking about the fire hazard the store represented. "How can you live with all this stuff? You should seriously consider getting rid of some of it."

"If I did, then I wouldn't have what you're looking for," she said calmly with her arms crossed over her chest, as if she'd said it a thousand times.

"Point taken."

Surprises

Our next Tour update was held Saturday night at the Blume house. Gloria was doing a tremendous job getting the Blume house ready. There had been a surprising amount of Christmas decorations stored up in the attic. Unfortunately, the nativity set and Santa and his reindeer Gloria remembered so fondly, were missing. There was no telling where they had gone or when.

I was shocked to see Jacob sitting with the ladies. Despite the forty degree weather, he was dressed in a track suit. "Um, Jacob good to see you. Are you volunteering with us now?"

He gave me a smirk and raised his chin at me. "Yup. I heard you need help and I just love the holiday season." He waved his hands expansively in the air as he spoke.

I gave him my best smile, no suspicion here, nope. Just me doing my job. "That's great. We already have all the houses assigned so I'll just pair you with someone..."

"Not to sound rude or anything but I heard Laurie Culpepper died, maybe I could take over her house?" All heads suddenly swiveled to look in his direction. Realizing his mistake, he tried again. "I mean, you're probably short on volunteers and I just want to help out my community."

Nice save there Jacob. "You know what? we could use some help on the Davis house. Sure, Gloria? Do you suppose you could take Jacob up there and introduce him to Emmeline? Maybe tomorrow morning?"

Gloria's face looked like she would just about eat him for dinner. Laurie had been her friend and I imagined Jacob's cavalier attitude irked her. She gave me a nod. "Okay, you two get together after the meeting." Jacob looked pleased with himself. If he was the thief, he would find out soon enough that Emmeline's house was the only one that had neither a Santa display nor a nativity scene.

"Alright ladies, and gentleman, how are everyone's houses coming along?"

Cindy raised her hand. "Cindy?"

"I have the Taylor's house in town. Last night someone stole Santa off the roof." She grimaced as she said it.

A queasy feeling began in my belly but quickly turned to anger. The thief was now messing with *my* houses. After the fiasco with the Fall Festival, I had hopes that this event would turn out better. I took a breath and smiled. "Anyone else having issues or thefts?"

Several hands rose into the air. I looked from face to face, catching Jacob looking surprised. Now that's weird. If he stole them would it be a surprise?

"I need all of you to file a report with Detective Smart. He's investigating the thefts." I scanned down the page of the tour updates. "Other than the thefts, we seem to be on track. Would someone please make a list of the missing items and I'll try to find replacements."

Tabitha Ward raised her hand. "Thank you Tabitha. Let's have our next meeting on Wednesday evening and we'll do a preview of the houses to see how they look." Tabitha settled back in her chair looking pleased with herself. She might be nearing ninety but she was a spry ninety. The other ladies all nodded in agreement. "Great. We'll meet back here, same time."

Meeting adjourned, I drove slowly home. A quick glance at the stolen items had revealed nothing in common. Some were old, some were new and they were from all over town. On a hunch I called Tabitha. "Do you know when the decorations were stolen? I didn't see it on the list."

"Let me see? I believe most of them were discovered missing when they went to put the decorations up."

"Thank you Tabitha." I disconnected the call by the button on the dash. They could all have been missing before the mess in the storage shed was discovered. Was it a decoy? The pieces had all looked new, which meant whoever it was had kept the old ones. Why? Had the sets from the Blume house also been stolen?

Crash

I was so wrapped up in my thoughts, at first I didn't notice the car behind me until it blinded me with its high beams in my rear view mirror.

I flipped the tab on the mirror to the dark view which helped for a bit. It had stopped snowing as I neared the gates to the entrance of the estates when the back end of my car was hit by the car behind me and spun me into a snow drift piled up on the side of the gate. My car was now facing the wrong way. Through the passenger window I could see a bundled figure coming towards me carrying a baseball bat.

Clearly this person meant me harm. Grabbing the door handle, I pushed it open only for it to stop after a few inches, stuck on the snow crushed up against it. With my heart racing, I desperately pressed on the window button. This time the window slid all the way down and I dove headfirst through the window ever so painfully slowly. More weight loss was definitely in my future.

A huge bang on the driver side of my car urged me on, slipping and falling in the snow. By this time the stranger was nearing the front of my car, so I hightailed it into the woods.

Okay, let's say I struggled to get into the woods. The branches on the trees were intertwined so tightly, it was difficult to make much headway. In frustration, I threw myself onto the ground and wriggled beneath the branches. The snow here was much thinner, probably due to the density of the branches and I was able to shimmy my way through. Snow filtered its ice cold fingers down my collar as a voice like a yeti, roared in frustration and the baseball bat made thwacking sounds as it slammed against the trees.

I was now cold, frightened and scared. Why was this figure after me? Was I on to something? Was it Jacob? Did he dig up Candace's backyard? Who else could it be? I didn't think I had annoyed anyone else that badly that they would want to kill me but you never know. People can be touchy nowadays.

Laying in the snow, I froze as the footsteps came closer. The bat slamming had stopped and I was afraid they would hear me move. Footsteps walked back and forth along the tree line. The bat would strike a branch randomly now and again. The figure never spoke a word; perhaps the voice would give them away and so I laid in the snow for what felt like forever, getting colder and wetter with every minute.

Sudden darkness surrounded me and I realized whoever it was had turned off my car and lights. Maybe it was just the illusion from the lights, but the darkness made me even colder and more afraid as I began shivering. The footsteps eventually walked away and I heard the other car door opening and closing. Unfortunately, the car never started up. They must be waiting for me to come out and get in my car.

With no other option, I squeezed farther into the bushes until I hit a wall. Literally, there was a wall here. Thankfully, there was also less snow and so I crawled on my hands and knees along the edge. Maybe it opened up at some point or perhaps I could get far enough away that I wouldn't be seen by the person in the vehicle.

This whole thing is crazy. Who would be that desperate to kill me? It had to be Jacob. I clearly had to rethink this whole sleuthing thing because this was definitely not fun. The other situations I had been in had had an exciting element to them. The danger had been a sudden thing where I had to act without thinking. Okay, so like this moment then. But there hadn't been any freaking snow.

I made a sudden decision that all future situations with imminent danger would not involve freezing or snow. Maybe the next dangerous situation could be in a tropical environment, like Hawaii, where I could wear cute clothes and catch some sun.

My knees were beginning to ache and my toes hurt. Thankfully, I had my gloves on but my hands were still freezing and little bits of dirt and pine needles were finding their way into my gloves and my boots. Grandmas were not designed for crawling. That should be left to babies with their cute chubby legs and arms.

Involuntarily, I let out a muffled expletive as my head hit another wall. In the near total darkness, I had no warning before it hit. I sat up and rubbed it vigorously to mitigate the pain as I contemplated my situation. First of all, what the heck was a wall doing here in the middle of nowhere hidden behind trees and with a corner, no less.

Why was someone stealing Santas and baby Jesus's? Who killed poor Laurie Culpepper? Wait, wait, wait, wait. Laurie just froze to death in the snow. Like Pete who was murdered. Is that why I was hung up on her death? It was not until that moment that I realized, that I did believe she had been murdered, call it a sixth sense or something. When had I become convinced? My mind raced as I thought back through the days.

I recalled the photos Patty had shown us. Maybe it was something in the pictures. I would have to look at them again. If I could ever get out of here.

Listening for a moment, there was nothing but silence. No animals or birds moved. Did that mean the car was still here or did they think I was a fox hunting them? Was the person gone? Did they leave when I wasn't paying attention or were they still there? Now I was angry at myself for not knowing. How could I be so stupid to not pay attention when my life was in danger? Some sleuth I was.

How far had I crawled anyway? Certainly far enough to hit a corner. Standing slowly, I felt up and down the wall hoping desperately to find some sort of opening. The wall went to the left, which meant I would eventually meet the road again and I certainly didn't want to go that way.

Backtracking didn't seem wise either, but I really had no other choice. Because of the wall there was a slight gap where the trees met the wall. My poor knees wished I had realized that sooner. Moving my hands up and down on the wall, I slowly retraced my steps, my heart pounding at every inch I moved back in the direction I had come from.

A sudden pain in my hip made me stop and run my hands over the wall there. It was some kind of knob. Really! A door in a wall that didn't belong here. What kind of nonsense is that? As soon as I got out, I was going to have to ask the mystery book club members about it. For now I turned the knob and pushed.

The door didn't budge so I leaned into it. When that didn't work, I took the risk of slamming my shoulder into it. It wasn't actually much of a slam because of the trees but it worked and the door moved a bit raising my hopes. A shower of snow cascaded down my neck, increasing my discomfort level. Stopping at my success, I listened again for any sound. Sound always seems to carry more at night and even more so in the snow.

At the sound of nothing, I tried once more and the door opened several inches, enough for me to squeeze through hoping there wasn't a sudden drop on the other side. At least on the other side, I might be able to use my light. Once through, I eased the door back in place until there was only a small gap that I could find with my fingers, if I needed to, in the darkness.

Except, it wasn't dark. The moon was rising from behind the trees. Out from under the cover of the leaves, the brilliant moonlight shone down. I gasped at the sight before me. There was an old paved road that wound down through the trees. It had been here long enough that the asphalt was cracked and broken, pieces missing here and there.

In wonder I looked back at the wall. The small door I had come through was clearly visible in the brick wall that had been erected over the road. Why would someone do that? And why didn't anyone know about this place? Taking a deep breath, I walked back over to the door and shut it completely. I hate when people don't shut the doors in the movies. That's how they always get caught. There was a knob on this side, I should be able to open it.

At this point in time, my only option was to follow the road. So I did. The road cutting through the trees created a river of light in the sky filled with stars. A rustle in the trees made me freeze in mid step as I watched a deer bound across the road. Birds flitted from branch to branch and small animals scurried through the underbrush. Was this an animal sanctuary? I felt like I was in Narnia, without the fur coats. I was still cold but the walking was warming me up. My watch showed that it was nearly midnight. I had been stuck out here for nearly an hour. Poor Ginger and Friendly would be wondering where their dinner was. The road finally ended at a small spring which was evident by the water pouring from the top of a square stone structure. It formed a small river that flowed under the trees.

Now what do I do? Go back and hope the car is gone? Surely, no one wanted me dead enough that they would still be waiting there. Of course, they had to be crazy in the first place to even want to kill someone. Did they kill Laurie? Ugh, the answer was in my brain, I just knew it, but unfortunately, it didn't want to surface. Trying not to think about it, only made me think about it more. That's when I spotted the small path going up the hillside. It looked pretty steep, but as there were no other options unless I wanted to wander aimlessly through the forest, never a good idea, I could check it out or go back. So I chose the path.

Whoever thought taking the road less traveled was a good idea, was wrong. This path wound around trees and back and forth, always climbing higher. Please, please, just let it lead to a shelter. Any kind of shelter would be nice.

My feet were sore, I was out of breath, and my lower back was beginning to ache when I found the only shelter, I didn't want. A dark cave opening was standing before me. The kind that bears like, or wolves. At this point, I turned on my phone flashlight because my feet were moving in that direction until I could see inside the dark recesses.

Bending down, I scanned the ground for animal tracks. Not finding any, kind of eased my mind until spiders entered it. Did caves have spiders? Do creepy crawlies hibernate? A sudden gust of cold wind made me think better of it and I ducked inside.

It was disappointingly small, no bigger than a large living room. Shining the light around, the walls were pretty, covered in dull gray stripes. It would make a beautiful counter top if it was polished. Perhaps it was some kind of quartz or granite. I put a small rock in my pocket so I could find out later.

The only thing in the cave was a small pile of wood and what I guessed was a flint. At least this would keep me warm until morning. If I could get it lit.

Okay, so it took like fifty tries, but I finally managed to light a fire. Mentally patting myself on the back, I took off my gloves and warmed my hands. At some point, I fell asleep, dreaming about Travis coming to rescue me. He was so worried when they found my abandoned car and with no answer to my calls on the phone or at home, he finally tracked me by my phone, finding the open door and…wait!

I awoke to cold and darkness. The fire had gone out. I sat up groaning. Every inch of my body was sore and my stomach was growling. Pulling out my phone, my heart sank at the sight of no signal. There would be no tracking my phone. "Oh no." I had shut the door completely. Would anyone find it? No. No one would go looking under trees for a wall that shouldn't be there.

They could track my footsteps. Except, that person had walked back and forth repeatedly. There wouldn't be any steps to find. I buried my face in my hands, feeling sorry for myself.

A plan

Ginger woke with a start, disturbing Friendly where she was curled up by her belly. Friendly hissed, irritated at having been awoken from her dream chasing mice.

"What's wrong?"

Ginger put her nose in the air and sniffed, then she padded from one room to the next. "Mom's not here and I'm hungry. Something's wrong."

"Just because you're hungry doesn't mean something's wrong," said Friendly. She leapt up onto the windowsill in the kitchen and peered out the window.

"Hey! You're not allowed up there."

"I'm a cat. I'm allowed wherever I want to go."

Ginger growled at the injustice of it. "What do you see?"

"The moon's pretty high, that means it's very late, or very early."

Ginger laid down and put her head on her paws. "Mom never forgets to feed me." She huffed a few times then came to a decision. "Maybe you should check the garage?" As soon as Friendly turned the corner in the hallway, Ginger got to her feet quietly and then slunk out the doggy door.

She shoved aside the bushes by the back fence and then crawled on her belly through the hole she had dug under the fence. Holly and Ben had stymied her efforts in jumping over the fence, but they hadn't found her hole in the ground.

On the other side, she cocked her ears so she looked like batman and sniffed the air. Already on high alert, she jumped straight in the air as Friendly walked between her legs.

"If you're going to sneak out then I am too," said the cat, watching Ginger sprawl on the ground when she landed.

"Mom will find out," growled Ginger.

"Won't Holly find out when we find her? That's where you're going right?" Ginger frowned. The cat had a point. "Okay. I guess you can come. Is it true that cats can see in the dark?"

Friendly sat down and licked a paw. "As a matter of fact, cats can see twice as good as dogs. But the moon is very bright so I can see even better."

"Great then let's go find Mom. You keep an eye out for an owl that can help us and I'll listen for any wolves or bears." Friendly continued to delicately lick her paw. "What are you waiting for?"

"I'm much smaller than you. I won't be able to keep up if you run."

Ginger shrugged. "Then maybe you should stay here."

"Ooorrr, you could carry me." Friendly looked pointedly at Ginger's large back. "Plus you're black and I'm black, so no one will see me."

Ginger's first instinct was to say no. Then she thought long and hard about the consequences of such an action. Cats were notoriously vindictive creatures and the results could be perilous.

Ginger tilted her head from side to side as if she was considering it and then finally relented. "Okay, but no claws. And I'm not responsible if you fall off."

"Of course not," Friendly said, her tiny nose held high as she sauntered over and leapt onto Ginger's back. She was a cat and therefore, had to uphold a cat's supercilious reputation but secretly, she liked Ginger more than a cat truly should. She was glad to have selected her for her sister. "Where are we going?"

"Mom said she was going to the Blume house, that's where Ben used to work. Bernard told me all about it. It's up the mountain through a tunnel."

"A tunnel?"

"Yes, there are lots of big houses there."

"I think I know what you're talking about. I'll tell you how to get there," purred Friendly.

Rescue

With a deep sigh, I sat up straighter and stretched a bit. I was just going to have to walk back out. I'd dug myself out of deeper situations before. This one just required a short walk to freedom.

Feeling better after my pep talk, I stretched a bit and then went to brave the cold with new found confidence. Plus, I really needed to pee.

Cold toilet seats have nothing on actual cold weather on a bare bottom. After taking care of business, I sat back down and waited for the sun to rise. The moon had set and there was no light. Sure, I could use my phone light, but that would run the battery down really quick plus one misstep and I would be down the hill faster than I wanted. So I waited huddled in the cold. Did I mention it was really really cold? A nice warm bear to snuggle up with would be great right about now. I wondered what Barney, the bear that had shown up at the Fall Festival, was doing. He'd looked kind of cute at the Fall Festival, sitting on his bottom eating pastries.

Or a warm person. Maybe the right warm person. A special one. Travis could be that right warm special person. Vana was right. Why was I pushing him away? What was I afraid of? Despite my winter clothing, I began to shiver.

My eyes kept drooping closed. I live in the snow, I know that that's a bad thing to do so I started running through all the things that needed to be done over the next few days. It always keeps me awake at night when I do want to sleep. It didn't work. The next I knew, I was dreaming of Barney coming to snuggle against me and keep me warm. The warmth and the fur under my fingers felt so real. Too real! My heart began pounding as I felt real fur under my fingers. Frozen in place, I slowly tried to peek through my eyelids. I knew this cave was a bad choice. Then Barney licked my face.

My eyes sprang open of their own accord at that point, sure I was about to die. "Ginger?" I burst out in shock.

Friendly was purring under my chin and Ginger was wriggling with glee and barking at me.

"Where did you guys come from? Oh, I'm so happy to see you!" I looked around puzzled at the lack of rescue vehicles. "How did you guys get in here?" My only response was more whimpers from Ginger and a few meows from Friendly. My beloved pets had kept me warm and saved my life. They were definitely getting special treats as soon as we got home. How they found me was a mystery to be solved later.

Getting to my feet, really slowly because my legs were stiff, I staggered over to the cave opening. A sudden cramp in my toes halted me until the pain subsided. Tentatively, I took a step and then another to ensure the pain wasn't coming back. Outside the cave, the first small ray of light began turning the eastern sky pink. I had survived the night.

The view from the mouth of the cave was spectacular. There was a whole valley spread out before me. It wasn't huge, maybe a mile from end to end and half a mile across, covered with trees. The valley floor rose up to meet sheer walls. Perhaps that was why it was overlooked, but still, why was it hidden? That wall was deliberate. And despite the door, no one had clearly entered here in a very long time.

The trip down the hill took less time and was much more pleasant than the trip up. For one thing, I had my pets with me. Friendly perched on my shoulder while Ginger pranced slowly through the snow. Birds were singing, I could hear the water babbling in the stream from the spring. There was a fresh scent to the air of pine trees and damp earth. I had to find out who this belonged to. This was just a mystery with no dead bodies. It might be fun to find the answer to this puzzle.

The shining sun displayed the wall in all its glory. Someone had taken the time to paint this side of the wall and the door to look like pine trees and forest vegetation to disguise it. I assume to hide it from the air. Paint was beginning to peel off displaying the bricks beneath and the door was the worse for wear, possibly because it was made of wood.

To get it open, I had to brace one foot on the wall and then pull the handle with both hands. It came open just precisely the same amount as it had the prior evening. Or was it early morning? I squeezed through and then waited for Ginger to follow me. I pulled it shut once again. There had to be other openings into this valley but maybe they were just too hazardous.

The worst part of the whole trip was having to squeeze back under the trees to get to the road. My body was now stiff and sore. My fingers barely worked. Without the adrenaline rush, forward movement was painstakingly slow. Ginger crawled along with me. The only one who really had it easy was the cat. By the time I was done, I was dripping with sweat and my arms and leg muscles were threatening to cramp. Apparently the adrenaline last night had allowed me to power through. I grabbed Ginger's collar and paused just inside the treeline. I could see my car sitting there quietly with the doors all shut. It was still facing the wrong way from when I had spun out.

I let Ginger go. She trudged to the car, lifting each foot high out of the snow before taking another step. She sniffed all around the car, then turned and barked at me. "What is it honey? Did you find something?"

My limbs all groaned in protest as I staggered to my feet. No other vehicles were around. Had no one come looking for me? My phone buzzed with incoming texts. One from Vana said, "Glad to hear you got home safely." Huh?

Without reading anymore, I hit the button to call her. "Vana, I'm so glad to hear your voice. Would you please come pick me up at the overpass to the estates? My car broke down and I'm freezing. I'll explain when you get here."

"I'm getting in my car now," she said, no questions asked. You had to love a friend who would drop everything for you. Honestly, I was afraid to get in my car. I was going to have it towed to a garage for a thorough going over. Who knew what that person might have done to it. I was nervous just standing out in the open in case that person came back so I went and stood behind a tree stamping my feet to stay warm with Ginger and Friendly until I saw Vana's car arrive.

As she pulled up behind my car, I dashed out from behind the tree and ran to the car. I let Ginger into the back seat and jumped in the front passenger seat. Vana's eyebrows rose at the sight of Ginger and the cat dashing through the snow to the car. Warmth never felt so good. Vana pulled away "Why are your dog and cat here?"

"They saved me. I was freezing and I woke up thinking it was Barney but it was my girls keeping me warm."

"Barney, the bear?"

"Yes, the bear. I didn't text you last night. How did you know I got home safely?"

Vana glanced over at me. "It was a group text message. Look in my phone and you'll see it." She reached into her purse and pulled it out, then unlocked it before handing it to me.

It was the first message. After a bunch of "me too" and "goodnight" texts it said, "it's Holly, I'm home safe, goodnight everyone."

I studied the text frowning and then looked at the phone numbers. There were ten different numbers, some with names attached and some without. "This wasn't me. Look, my name doesn't even show up. I think that was the point of the group text, so you wouldn't notice."

Vana sighed. "I'm sorry Holly, that's exactly what happened. I didn't even look to see, I just assumed you added me accidently. I did think it was weird that you sent it. You never tell me you're home safe." Vana looked at me. "What happened last night? And why are your pets here?"

"Hey! Eyes on the road." Once she was paying proper attention to the road once more, I began my tale. "Someone tried to kill me last night." I filled her in on all the details. She was after all my sister in everything but blood relation.

"This isn't good," she said as she navigated into her driveway.

"You're telling me it's not. And that valley, what's up with that? And that wall? What are we doing at your house?" I asked, finally taking notice of our location.

Vana pulled into her garage, shut off the engine and turned in her seat to look at me. "Seriously Holly? Someone just tried to kill you, you were trapped in a cave all night and you are concerned about a mystery valley?" Her voice rose sharply at the end. "You're staying here until we check out your house and make sure everything is okay. You're going to go in my house and take a hot shower while I call Travis and have him check out your house." She pulled the key out of the ignition, grabbed her purse and climbed out of the car. She was right and wrong. No one would mess with my house with Ginger inside but that still didn't mean that someone wasn't waiting for me outside. Obviously, I was dealing with someone deranged.

"No one would mess with my house with Ginger there," I pointed out.

"Except, she's not," and she pointed her finger at my dog who was currently relieving herself in the snow.

I chewed on my bottom lip as I let that sink in. "Fine. But I want hot coffee. Lots of it."

"Deal," she said and smacked her hand on the roof of the car. "Now let's get inside, it's cold."

Let me tell you, nothing feels as good as a hot shower when you've spent the night in the cold. I stood under the stream and gradually raised the hot water temperature until I was enveloped in clouds of steam. Vana left me some cozy sweats to put on and had a cup of hot coffee waiting for me as I stepped out of the bathroom door.

She had already made some bacon and eggs for Ginger and Friendly. "Travis is on his way to your house and sent a tow truck for your car. He'll come by afterwards." She settled me on her comfy white couch with a plush blanket and then left to make breakfast. Fatigue settled into every inch of my body as I leaned back against the pillow and then promptly fell asleep.

I awoke hours later to a wet kiss. Ginger was wriggling in excitement before me with Travis unsuccessfully trying to pull her back by her collar.

Travis's face lit up with a beautiful smile. "I think she likes me. And the bits of steak I brought didn't hurt either."

I snuggled my hero dog until she settled down. I struggled to sit up without groaning. I ached in every part of my body. Oddly, the worst pain was where my seat belt had restrained me during the spin out.

"Are you okay?" He asked, concern etched on his handsome features. He sat down in an overstuffed leather recliner at my affirmation. "Your house is fine. I couldn't find any evidence of anyone trying to break in."

He took a deep breath before continuing. "Now your car is a different story. Someone cut the brake line. He studied my face for a moment and I squirmed under his glare. "Why does someone want you dead?" His question filled me with dread.

Shaking my head, I said, "I've been asking around about the missing Santas and baby Jesus's," I said shrugging.

"Santas and baby Jesus?" Vana had just walked into the room with a tray holding coffee cups and an insulated pitcher. She set it down on the glass coffee table and dispensed the cups all around. "Could it be Bonnie?"

Her question filled me with dead. Could it be Bonnie? "The person was bundled up and it was dark." I pressed my lips together and found myself shaking my head slowly. "I think she's too smart for that. This person was angry, really angry. Bonnie is cold and calculating."

"I'll still look into her alibi for last night," said Travis.

I filled the two of them in on my investigation so far. That niggling feeling kept poking at my brain but every time I tried to concentrate on it, it slipped away again. "Travis, was there anything weird about Laurie Culpepper's death?"

He looked at me curiously, "Why do you ask?"

"Several of the ladies keep comparing it to Pete's death and I'd really like to put their minds at ease." I could see him mulling his answer over.

"No. Looks like she slipped and fell and then froze in the snow. Her hip was fractured so she likely couldn't get help. She was found in the afternoon by a neighbor out walking their dog."

Laurie was a real estate agent, so nothing out of the ordinary. At her age, falling was just one of the risks. I rubbed my forehead with my fingers. The Holiday Tour was coming up quickly and there was still so much to be done. I didn't need these distractions.

"I need to check in with Joe at the office. Maybe Wendy has some Santas we could purchase to replace the stolen ones." My mind began racing with all of the tiny details that still needed to be done. I looked to Vana, "Can you take me to get a rental?"

"No."

"If we go right now...wait, what? No?"

"No. I'll be your driver today. Someone tried to kill you last night and might have succeeded if not for Ginger." Ginger looked up at her name and Friendly meowed. "And the cat. What's her name?"

I grabbed my cup of coffee and took a sip as I mumbled her name into the cup.

Travis cocked his eyebrows. "Did you say Friendly?"

Vana repeated the name and then began laughing. "Are you really yelling, 'Friendly,' out the door? I can't imagine what your neighbors think."

I set my cup down and glared at each of them. "She picked it. I tried lots of other names, Ebony, Soot, Max." At the mention of Max, she hissed at me. "See? She chose it. What could I do?" I threw my hands in the air.

Vana was laughing so hard she was crying and Travis was failing at keeping a straight face. "Oh, well if the cat chose it, okay."

I huffed out a breath. "And I should probably figure out how Ginger's getting out." Ginger sat up and her little brown eyebrow dots rose up in surprise. '

"Maybe that's not such a good idea," said Travis. "She has saved you a few times now." He reached over and gave her back a good scratching. I twisted my lips thinking. It was true, she'd tried to save me when the intruder broke in at Mildred's which is how I found out she was jumping over the fence.

"Maybe you're right, but I don't want her to get hurt."

Travis held Ginger's face in both of his hands and looked into her eyes. "Ginger. You can't escape the yard anymore unless you're going to rescue someone. Okay?" To my surprise, she gave a little woof and then licked Travis's face. "See? She agrees," he said. "So it's all settled. Vana will take you and the girls home and I'll go investigate the Christmas thefts." He bit his lower lip. "And I might just visit the coroner and take a second look into Laurie's death. The ladies have been making comments to me also. Perhaps I can set their minds at ease."

I rolled my eyes at him. "Glad to hear it's not just me they're harassing. Do you know they woke me up at 2 am to go look at where she died?"

"You did what now?" he asked. Oops.

114

"Would you look at the time. I really should be getting these animals out of Vana's hair. They're probably tired and there's so much work to do. Joe's taking his real estate test this week, and I've got several transactions that are closing soon." I grabbed his arm and escorted him to the door. Thanks for coming by Travis, I'll see you later." Then, not knowing what else to do, I gave him a peck on the cheek. Then froze and slowly shut the door in his surprised face.

Vana's eyebrows were all the way up to her hairline. "What? I just gave him a friendly kiss like you would to a friend."

"You just shut the door in his face."

"Oh. Oops?"

Mom

Vana pulled into my driveway and that was when I realized that in all the excitement, I had left my purse in my car and had no keys to get in. Now was when I wished my garage had a key code.

I sighed loudly and grit my teeth. Vana looked at me puzzled. "I'm going to have to crawl through the doggy door." She raised her eyebrows at me just as someone banged on the car door window and made me jump.

"Mom!" My mother was standing outside the car with an anxious look on her face. I clutched my chest to still my pounding heart.

"Holly! There was a man snooping around your house earlier. Who was it? And where were you all night?"

I motioned to Vana to put the window down. "Mom, what are you doing here?

"The twins called me to tell me about the *guy* and I hurried over as quickly as I could but you were. not. here." She looked at me sternly through the window.

That's when I noticed my front door was open. "How did you get in the house?"

"I crawled through the dog door of course. You never gave me a key. What did you think I was going to do, break in?"

"Um, you kinda just did that," I pointed out. "Which is exactly why I didn't give you a key in the first place. You're always overstepping your boundaries, mom!"

I felt Vana tapping me on the shoulder and looked her way. "Do you suppose we could continue this argument inside? It's getting rather cold out here."

I frowned at my mom. "Mom, this is Vana. We are coming in and you are leaving," I said as I opened the car door.

"Now that you're here, we should go get some breakfast together. I haven't gotten to spend any time with you." She put a pouty look on her face, conveniently ignoring everything I just said.
Ginger and Friendly ran past us into the house.

"Did you change that cat's name yet? Did she tell you she named that cat Friendly?" she added to Vana, then turned back to me. "I don't know what you were thinking, sticking your head out the door and calling 'Friendly' for the whole neighborhood to hear."

Shutting the door behind me and enjoying the warmth of the living room, I took a moment to respond. I love my mother but I left home a long time ago because of this behavior from her. Besides, I'm in my fifties, way beyond the age where I need to have my behavior corrected. We should have a relationship as peers.

"Mom, I need to change and get ready for work. But first, Mildred's twin sisters? How do you know them?" I turned my curious eyes on her and waited expectantly, hoping for the truth.

She sniffed deeply through her nose and tossed her short hair.

I squinted my eyes at her suspiciously.

"We ran into each other at the hotel, if you must know. Your friends set me up with that 'delightful' man," she said the word sarcastically and I waited for the punch line. "He only wanted free food." I groaned inside. Apparently, paying the man to date my mother didn't include him paying his own way. Darn! A good date could have kept her out of my hair for a very long time.

"Anyway, they are the most interesting women although they do bicker quite a bit. They've told me all about this town and everyone in it."

I could hear Vana in the kitchen making coffee. My mom went to the couch and made herself comfortable. Too comfortable. I narrowed my eyes and looked at her suspiciously. "They told me all about that deplorable Bonnie Belmar. Oh, my poor sweet girl. I won't let that nasty woman hurt you ever again. Come and sit down next to mommy." She patted the seat cushion next to her.

"Mom. What's going on? Why are you really here?"

She puckered her lips and pouted again. "Can't I come and see my daughter for Christmas?"

I bit my lip and dropped on to the chair farthest away from my mother. "What happened?" I asked in a resigned voice.

"Nothing, nothing. It's just your sister doesn't understand me. I try to be helpful and she doesn't appreciate anything I do."

I could imagine what her help entailed. I sighed inside knowing I was going to regret my next question. My mom was the result of her upbringing. She was an only child and her mother was the ultimate helicopter mother before that was even a thing. She really didn't know how not to interfere. "What happened mom?"

My mom's voice got teary and her eyes actually watered. "She kicked me out and now refuses to let me live with her. How ungrateful can you be? I was in labor for 20 hours with her and this is the thanks I get?"

"Mom. you gave her dog away and rearranged her house, then you called the police on her husband when he came home at two in the morning. What did you think was going to happen?"

She sniffed and shrugged. "He shouldn't have been coming home so late, or so early, whatever." She spun her hand in the air.

"He was coming home from work," I said sternly. I took a deep breath and then blew it out. "Okay, I'll find you a place to stay. Perhaps there's a cabin for rent around here. I know there's some nice apartments in town." For the sake of *my* dog and cat, she certainly wasn't staying here.

"It's okay honey, the twins said I could stay with them."

My mouth opened and closed a few times before I managed to speak. "Mildred's sisters, who are visiting Mildred, said you could move into Mildred's house?" My eyebrows rose higher as the words left my lips.

Vana pressed a coffee cup into my hands and whispered into my ear, "it has the special sweetner," then handed a cup to my mom.

"Thank you, Vana was it?" She asked.

Vana smiled and retreated back to the kitchen. I sipped my cup and tasted the rum then took another drink, as the alcohol warmed me from the inside. The twins and my mom can't just take over poor Mildred's house, plus, the three of them living that close to Mildred and I would be an absolute nightmare. We would never have any peace.

That brought up another thought, did I want Mildred to live here? Did she want to? My brows drew down together. Where was she last night? I pulled out my phone and punched in her number.

"Mildred." Relief spread through my body when she answered. "Are you okay? You didn't come home last night."

"Holly, I'm sorry. I got my apartment back in town. I didn't want to keep putting you out. I called you last night and left a message."

I hadn't listened to my messages. "That's fine, Mildred. When did you decide this?"

"Caroline came into the candy store yesterday. She owns the apartments, and I told her all about my sisters and she let me know the last tenants had left and I could have it if I wanted. I do love my little house, but being in town in the winter time is actually a good thing for me. I hope you don't mind?"

"Not at all Mildred. You do what is best for you. I'll talk to you later." I disconnected the call. My battery showed five percent and I went into the kitchen to plug it in, amazed that it still had any juice. My mom remained on the couch sipping her coffee, but I caught her glancing at me over the rim and then pretending she wasn't.

"Thanks for the coffee Vana, I needed that," I murmured over the rim of my cup.

She gave me a smile as she leaned against the counter and sipped her own cup of coffee. I gave her a pointed look and then looked at her cup. "Don't worry, I only put it in your cup. What are you going to do with your mom when we leave?"

"Can we drop her off at the...hmmm, I'm not sure where she's going," I said, suddenly confused.

Vana pushed away from the counter. "Don't worry, I got this." She walked into the living room and sat down next to Doris. "Doris, it's so nice to meet you. Holly's going to get changed for work and then we're going into town. Do you want to be dropped off at the hotel or Mildred's house?"

My mom's face froze as she realized she'd just been outmaneuvered. "I uh, I suppose I should go to Mildred's. The twins will be expecting me.

A puzzle

Wendy said that she did in fact have a few large Santas that we could purchase. She agreed to hold them if I paid in advance, which I did. Vana borrowed her husband's truck and we made the short drive to Morecroft to pick them up.

Vana pulled around to the back of the shop and shut off the truck. Raised voices could be heard coming from inside the store. A few moments later, Wendy came out the shop's back door.

"I saw you drive past the front window," she said in explanation. "The Santa's are in the garage." She was dressed in the most outlandish Christmas sweater and I deliberately chose not to comment on it. She unlocked the door and raised the garage door. Three 4-foot Santas were lined up just inside.

"We're you having a problem with a customer?" I asked.

Wendy grimaced. "Just Jacob. He's been harassing me about Santa's, said he wants one for his rooftop display but I told him they were already sold. He doesn't like to take no for an answer."

"He doesn't happen to wear track suits does he?"

Wendy looked surprised. "Yes. How did you know?"

Vana and I looked at each other. "He lives in Appleby. I've run into him a few times. He...has issues. Was there anything else he was interested in?" It would be highly suspicious if he was also looking for baby Jesus.

Wendy shook her head no. "Just Santa."

"I do appreciate you holding these for us. Someone stole some from our Christmas displays. Probably kids messing around but our Holiday Tour of Homes is a fundraiser and people will be expecting to see Santa and his reindeer."

"Yeah, you should come," added Vana. "It's December 23rd from 6-9 pm. The lights look better in the dark and there will be food."

Actually, I already bought tickets. My mom and I go every year." Wendy patted one of the Santas after placing it in the back of the truck. " I'm glad to know my Santas are going to have a good home."

We stopped at an old country store on the way home for a cup of hot chocolate. I ran inside while Vana waited in the truck. The cashier was an old man who should have probably retired a long time ago. His hair was white and he moved as slowly as his old cash register worked. There was only one other woman in the store when we entered and she was already at the counter.

"Sorry ma'am, you're two pennies short." He rested his palms on the counter and waited for her to come up with the two cents. She was only buying a small carton of milk.

"I'll pay for it," I said and offered my credit card.

He tapped on the counter. "Read the sign. We don't take cards here. Cash only."

"Fine." I began digging through my pockets for some change, depositing the detritus in my pockets on the counter—an old tissue, a piece of gum and some business cards with bent edges. The rock from the hidden valley slipped from my fingers and bounced on the counter.

"You know what?" I heard him say. "Go ahead, but bring me two cents the next time you come in." Which was a good thing because I did not in fact have any change.

The woman gratefully promised and scurried to the door before he changed his mind. "And don't tell anyone I did this," he yelled.

"Wouldn't want people to start expecting handouts."

"Oh, wow, yeah," I said. "That would be terrible."

Ignoring me he picked up the rock I had dropped. "Where'd you get this?" He snapped at me suspiciously.

"I found it on the ground."

"I don't think so," he said, thrusting the rock in front of my face.

"Why? What is it?" I asked, backing up a step.

He narrowed his eyes at me and a tingle of fear ran up my spine. "I know where you got it. How'd you get in there? You'd better keep that information to yourself or there will be trouble."

Grabbing the rock, I dashed out the door.

"Secrets are secrets for a reason!" He yelled after me.

Jumping in the car, I slammed the door closed and then pressed the lock down. "Let's go," burst from my lips. Vana shifted into drive and sped from the gas station.

"You okay?" she asked a mile down the road.

"Yes, just drive please."

Pursing her lips, she said. "sooo, no hot chocolate?" Glancing over at her, I burst out laughing, releasing the tension from my body. After all, he was just an old man, what trouble could he cause?

Once I could breathe normally, I filled her in on the creepy man behind the counter as she drove us home.

"What do you think he means?" I finally asked.

"The easy answer would be to find out what that rock is. You should take it to a geologist. There's probably one at the college in Morecroft." She picked up the rock from my hand. "Were there more rocks like this?"

"The whole cave was like this. What do you think it means?"

"I think trouble has a habit of finding you."

I couldn't argue with that.

Questions

Caroline's home was one of the ones missing a Santa and Vana and I drove straight there to let her pick the one she wanted. I shivered a little as we drove under the bridge where my car was struck.

"You okay?" asked Vana.

"I know this is weird, but would you mind driving through the bridge again?" She gave me a side eye but did it. We drove slowly under the rather long bridge, turned around and drove back through in the direction we were originally going.

"The door I went through led to a road. I think the bridge is so deep because there was originally a road here."

"What are you talking about?"

"Why is there even an underpass here?"

"Obviously because they cut it through a mountain."

"Did they?"

Vana looked at me then pulled off on the side of the road and stopped the truck. We both got out and looked back the way we had come. On the left side, the mountain gently sloped down to the bridge but on the right side the dirt came down in a small hill from the top and then ended in a bunch of trees.

Vana shrugged. "Maybe it's just decorative?"

"Okay, but why is it so deep? It's at least twenty feet." I walked to the underpass and examined the ground. Following the wall around the side. The bushes were impossibly thick to get through.

"Plants don't grow thick like this naturally," said Vana thoughtfully. "It's almost like someone planted them here.

"I think the road connected with this one. Someone deliberately blocked it with this bridge."

Vana stamped her feet on the ground. "You may be right but my feet are starting to freeze. Can we get going?"

"You see the dilemma of course?"

"The dilemma of frozen feet?" she snarked.

I chose to ignore her comment. "The valley has clearly been deliberately hidden. How am I supposed to know who to ask about the secret without giving it away?"

"You don't even know that it is a secret. Someone could have just built up to the edge of someone else's property."

"Cutting off all access? That road was paved!"

Vana jingled her keys. "I'm leaving. If you're not in the car in 30 seconds, I will leave you here. Contemplate that."

Jacob

J acob called me while I was preparing to conduct my final check of the tour homes. We'd managed to secure enough replacements to complete everyone's Christmas sets. As long as there were no more thefts, that is.

"Holly? I don't think this is going to work out for me. Emmeline already has everything done. Perhaps there's someone who still needs help?"

His call deepened my suspicion that he had something to do with the thefts. "I'm really sorry Jacob, but everyone already has their assignments. I'm afraid Emmeline's was the only vacancy. I still need you there to host the night of the event. Now I've really got to get going, Gloria's waiting for me at the Blume house."

"What are you doing up there?" he asked.

"Didn't you hear? We're ending the tour at the Blume house. We're going to have a big Christmas display set up outside."

"Do you really think that's a good idea? It's going to be awfully cold outside. I don't think that's a very good plan."

"I'm sorry Jacob, I really do have to go."

"But Holly, Emmeline has the Nightmare before Christmas up. That's really a sacrilege to the true meaning of Christmas. There's not even a nativity scene here. I can't be a part of such an anti-Christian display.

"Why Jacob, I had no idea you were so religious."

When he spoke again, the offense came clearly through the line. "I'll have you know I'm a devout Catholic."

"I'm sorry Jacob. I didn't mean to offend you. Let me see if there's someone that will replace you."

"Thank you. That's all I'm asking." The line went dead leaving me to wonder what he was up to.

Jacob was religious, go figure. It was then I realized what had been bothering me about the storage unit with all the broken Santas. There were no broken baby Jesus's. If someone was searching for something hidden inside, why weren't the baby Jesus's broken? Unless, you were afraid to because of your religion. Like a devout Catholic. I was going to need to investigate Jacob's house.

Book club

"Ladies, we need to get to the bottom of these Christmas thefts." I had gathered the ladies together to discuss our mysteries. "We might wake up on the day of the tour and discover missing pieces. We've already had to replace several Santas. Thankfully the nativity scenes are all inside."

"What did you have in mind Holly?" asked Mildred.

I paced back and forth in my living room. "What does Santa and baby Jesus have in common?"

"Oh, oh, they both give you gifts," said Cindy with her hand halfway in the air. "One gives the gift of life and the other gives gifts of things if you're good."

"One's tiny, one's big," said Maggs with a shrug.

Those are differences," I said thoughtfully. "What do they have in common besides gifts?"

"They're both hidden," commented Mildred. "One in your heart and one in the North Pole."

I stopped suddenly and spun to stare at her. "Or, or not," she faltered. "I guess Santa is sometimes seen?"

"No. Mildred, I think you might be on to something. Could there be something hidden inside the Santas?"

"Oooh, all those broken Santas we found in the shed." Mildred's eyes grew big.

I waved my hand back and forth in front of my face. "I don't think so. I think that was a ruse to throw us off. The pieces all looked like they were from new Santas not old faded ones." Could something really be hidden inside? But what?

"It doesn't make sense," I said, thinking out loud. The Santas are huge and Jesus is so small. What could possibly be the connection?"

"Did you find anything out about Laurie?" asked Gloria.

I pressed my lips together into a thin line and shook my head. "Travis believes it was an accident but he said he would take another look. Did you ladies find anything?"

"I've found the decorations for the Blume house but not the nativity or Santa and his eight reindeer. I'll keep looking."

"I meant about Laurie or the Christmas thefts," I said quickly to forestall another argument with Maggs.

"Do you know what's strange?" began Cindy without raising her hand first, which was strange. "Whenever I mention Christmas and the Blume house to the old folks, they suddenly clam up."

I bit my lip to keep from laughing, as if she wasn't old herself at age 72. Managing to get myself under control, I said, "That is weird. The tour is almost here. Why don't we focus on helping Gloria with the Blume house. Maybe the answers will come if we aren't looking for them."

The ladies reluctantly agreed. Even if we didn't find the nativity and Santa sets, the Blume house would still look spectacular.

Not a birthday

The phone rang and I let out an audible sigh when I saw Gloria's name displayed on the screen.

"Who's dead?" was how I answered the phone.

"No one's dead. This isn't a murder mystery," declared Gloria defensively. "We just have a bit of an issue at Caroline's house and need you to get here right away."

"Gloria, it's nine o'clock at night, why is anyone there?"

Gloria's voice took on a petulant tone. "You know how she is. Please just get here right away."

"Fine, I'll be there in twenty minutes." I disconnected and grabbed my coat and purse. Ginger whined as she saw me preparing to leave. "It's okay, girl. I'll be right back." I debated taking her, but Caroline would have a fit if I brought a dog to her house.

As I drove through the snow, the words of Clement Clarke Moore's *'Twas the Night Before Christmas* came to mind. The light of the full moon really did give the "luster of mid-day to objects below." It made me wonder if there was going to be a full moon for Christmas this year. Would I be able to see the reindeer from Santa's sleigh? Probably not if someone kept stealing the Santas. What on earth could someone possibly want with decades old Santas?

The lights were all blazing at Caroline's house as I pulled into the drive. I stepped out into the freezing air, tightening the scarf around my neck and hustled to the front porch.

The door opened and Gloria popped onto the porch. "Thank you for coming so quickly," she said as she pulled me inside.

My heart dropped to my feet as a chorus of voices yelled, "Happy birthday!"

The voices died down at my look of bewilderment. "It's not my birthday," I finally said, confused. The ladies all looked at each other, confused as well.

Maggs's face took on a disgusted look. "I told you we shouldn't have believed her."

"Why would she lie?" questioned Caroline, which confused me even further because she had been keeping her distance from us 'underlings.' Why was she throwing me a party? Alma grimaced and gave Caroline's arm a reassuring squeeze.

Cindy's polite voice cut through the noise. "I tried to tell you she couldn't be trusted."

I clapped my hands to get their attention through the bickering. "Who are you talking about?"

Silence reigned for thirty seconds, then Gloria stepped forward. "Bonnie. She told Alma and Caroline that it was your birthday. She said she was trying to make amends."

And there it was. Bonnie was back to her usual meddlesome self. Well, I for one, wasn't going to let her have the win on this one.

"You know what? I don't mind. Let's call this Holly's belated birthday party. Now, is there cake?"

The cake was absolutely delicious, I had never tasted anything like it. "Caroline, where ever did you get this cake from?" I asked, before shoving another bite in my mouth.

"I'm glad you like it. I have it shipped in from New York. I buy only the best," she said with the air you would expect from someone rich who always gets what they want.

An hour later we were all full of cake and coffee and I began to make my goodbyes. Caroline was standing in the hall, perhaps hoping we would get the hint and leave. "Caroline, I'm sorry Bonnie said that to you but thank you for hosting my birthday at your house."

"Of course, it was no problem at all. I was happy to do it," she said. "I heard that poor woman is going to be buried this weekend. It's so terrible what happened to her."

I smiled politely, "Yes, Laurie was a wonderful person."

"She's going to be buried in that beautiful blue dress she wore at the Christmas party," said Mildred from behind me. She put her hand to her cheek. "Oh, dear, I should have taken the jewelry with me. What was I thinking?"

"It's okay, Mildred," I said, putting my arm around her shoulder. "I'm sure that tomorrow will be fine."

"Are you really going to bury her with jewelry on?" asked Caroline aghast. "Don't you think that will be an invitation to thieves?"

"I'm sure it will be fine," said Mildred. "It's not as if they're valuable. She got them at a craft fair."

"Oh, I guess that's all right then," said Caroline. "I do you hope you enjoyed your non-birthday."

"I did. It was fun." I hesitated, wanting to warn her but not sure of her relationship with Bonnie. "Caroline, I hope you won't be offended but Bonnie isn't a very...trustworthy person. Please double check anything she tells you."

Caroline grimaced before replying. "Yes, I can see that now."

Clues

I was safely ensconced behind my desk researching home prices in the estates. I don't know why I did it but on a whim, I looked up the information on Caroline's house.

This can't be right. I looked at the figures again. It showed Caroline was mortgaged to the hilt. This was interesting information but not relevant to the task at hand. I rubbed my eyes and tried to refocus. Other thoughts intruded and refused to let me work. What was up with that rock? I fished it out of my purse and bounced it a few times in the palm of my hand. It felt like a rock. It looked like granite. Vana had said to take it to a geologist's office.

A sparkle caught my eye and I rolled it around in my palm. maybe it had gold in it. I needed to find out if there was a geologist at Morecroft College. Perhaps Joe would take it for me, then there would be no connection to me.

A knock at the door interrupted my thoughts so I quickly slipped the rock back into my purse.

"Come in," I called.

A beautiful woman entered the room. "Can I help you?" I asked politely.

A giggle passed her lips and she suddenly squealed, "I passed my test!"

Huh? "Are you sure you have the right place?" She looked vaguely familiar. In my business, I try to remember faces but I couldn't place hers.

She plopped herself down in the chair in front of my desk, leaned her arms on the edge and then rested her chin in her hands.

"Joe?" I asked, shocked. I had never seen my assistant as anything other than a guy.

"Yes!" she exclaimed. "I passed my real estate exam and you inspired me. Bonnie almost ruined my life and I figured maybe I needed a chance. I thought I'd try to be my real self for a while. I know my sister will love it."

"You know that I will support you whatever you want to do Joe. Do I still call you Joe?" I asked.

"Yes, but J o, no e. I have to thank you Holly. You've showed me that women can make it in a man's world." She shrugged. "If I'm going to be a fulltime agent, I want to do it as the real me."

"Wow Jo, that's great." Then I realized what she'd said. "Wait. Full time?"

Jo bit her bottom lip. "So you did catch that. I've loved being your assistant and I'll help you find another one, but I feel like I need to stop hiding behind other people and make my own way in the world."

I got up from my seat and went around the desk to give her a hug. "I'm happy for you Jo, but I'm still sad to lose you."

Scrunching up her face she asked, "will you still help me?"

"Of course I will," I exclaimed. "I love helping people succeed. Anything you need, I'm here." I pursed my lips. "Speaking of needing, I have an errand for you, if you don't mind, but it needs to remain on the down low."

"Sure Holly, what is it?"

Retrieving the rock from my purse, I put it in an envelope and handed it to her. "I need this taken to a geologist. This rock is at the bottom of a mystery and I need to find out what it is."

Jo bounced the envelope in the palm of her hand. "Sure thing. I'm going that way tomorrow." She stashed it in, what I have to say, was a most gorgeous handbag. "Alright then, I'll just be off to work. Thanks again Holly."

Deciding to take a break, I donned my jacket and made my way down the street to Mildred's candy shop. The little bell above the door tinkled as I entered the store. The delicious aroma of popcorn assailing my nostrils as I stepped inside.

Mildred was helping a customer at the register so I perused the candy displays while waiting my turn. The beep of the card machine signaled the end of the transaction and I greeted Mildred with a smile.

"How's the twins?"

"Oh no, don't say that word, they might show up."

"Ah, the name that must not be said, like in Harry Potter and the Lord of the Rings."

Mildred shook her head sadly. "They are as thick as thieves with your mother. I'm sure they're up to something," she said with a grimace. I couldn't even imagine what my mother was doing with the two sisters who constantly bickered. She always hated it when my sister and I would fight.

"So what can I get you?" Mildred's question interrupted my reverie.

"I'll have a pumpkin spice latte. It is the season after all. What's with the popcorn?" I asked, glancing over at the old fashioned popcorn machine in the corner that was churning out popped corn.

"I thought I'd make some popcorn balls for the tour. You know, red and green."

"Sounds delicious," I said, my stomach suddenly hungry. The door tinkled as someone came in.

Mildred crossed over to the popcorn machine and filled a bag. Steam was still rising from the top when she handed it to me. "On the house." She squinted her eyes as she looked into my face. "You look tired."

I blew a heavy breath out through my lips. "I've been researching comps around Caroline's house." Lowering my voice, I added, "I'm surprised she just remortgaged her house with the interest rates so high."

"Oh, that's not good." Mildred clamped her hand over her mouth and then spoke over the top of it in a whisper. "I heard her husband just lost his job. Poor thing." Mildred would call a shark a poor thing.

"Perhaps that explained her attitude," I said. Although it was incredibly nice of her to host a birthday party for me.

"Oh, no. She's always been that way. She would be absolutely horrified if she knew you knew about her finances. I don't know how her husband puts up with her to be honest."

Mildred handed me my latte and I took a sip. Spicy yumminess burned my tongue. "What time is the committee meeting tonight?"

"Six o'clock on the dot, " I said.

Updates

My living room was filled with women. Apparently we were missing Jacob this evening. The ladies were all chit chatting about various things when I heard Tabitha say as clear as day. "She's going to have to sell her house and downsize."

"Oh my," said Cindy. "Caroline is a very particular person, everything she buys is of the finest quality. I can't believe she'll have to buy cheap." This was the first time I actually saw someone make the eek emoji face with her teeth showing.

"You guys are crazy," interjected Maggs. "She'll die before she lets anyone think she can't afford 'the best.'" As she said it, she tossed her hair back with her hand and stuck her nose in the air. The other ladies disguised their laughter at the dead on impression as a sudden coughing fit.

"Ladies, now really. Are we gossiping at Christmas time?" I admonished them. "We need to get our houses wrapped up for the tour. How is everybody doing?"

Tabitha stood up. "My house is done. Thank you for the Santa. Houses 1-4 will have hors d'oeuvres, houses 5-8 will have sandwiches and fruit, and houses 9-12 will have desserts. Then we'll meet at the Blume house to give out gifts and sing carols." She sat down and muttered "hopefully Barney's sleeping," under her breath.

"Thank you Tabitha. Gloria, how's the Blume house coming along?"

"It would really help if I could get those pictures of the previous celebrations," she grumped and looked pointedly at the other ladies who ducked their eyes away and pretended to be interested in something else.

Putting my hands on my hips, I addressed the group. "You all were supposed to ask around town and see if anyone remembered the holidays at the Blume house? What happened?"

Cindy raised her hand. "Oh, we did, but they all say they don't remember. I even went to the old timers breakfast at the Blume house. Did you know they are trying to have the Blume house declared a historical monument?"

Gloria flailed both her hands in the air. "Do you see what I have to work with? It would help if the nativity scene was intact but according to a note I found, all the pieces were split up and sent home with different families."

"They what?" I asked.

"Split up. Different families. I heard it clear as day," said Maggs. Ignoring her, I addressed Gloria.

"Did the note have the names of the families involved?" I asked.

Gloria scratched her head as she thought. Then shook it. "Nope. There was a list of each item. Your usual eight reindeer, Santa, Jesus and the Wisemen, Mary and Joseph, an angel and a star."

"Should be nine reindeer," cut in Maggs. I gave her a 'what the heck' mom look. "You know, Rudolph."

"Oh yes," said Cindy. "Everybody forgets about him."

"He only just did it for the one night," said Patty.

"Besides the harness only has slots for eight reindeer," added Mildred.

When did I lose control of the committee? Leaving them to discuss the semantics of the reindeer, I retired to the kitchen to refill my coffee cup. I contemplated adding a little something extra to it, but the angel on my shoulder talked me out of it.

Besides, something was bugging me about the whole situation. Is that what was buried behind Carol's old house? An old Santa? The red paint flakes certainly fit and the previous owner, he acted a little strange when I asked him about it. Jacob had been arguing with Wendy about selling the Santas to us. Why did he want them? Did Alma know something?

"Holly!" yelled the ladies all together.

"Yes?"

"We've been calling you," said Maggs. "I understand why you're ignoring us though."

"I'm not," I began and then thought better of it. "Are you all ready to continue? Or do we need to discuss the reindeer some more? I can wait."

"No need to get snarky," said Gloria. "That's Maggs's job."

The doorbell rang and I paused the meeting to answer it only to find Travis on my doorstep with two other officers. "Holly Holcraft?" said the taller one with ginger hair.

"Yes? What's going on?" I looked at Travis and he mouthed 'I'm sorry' to me.

The shorter, stocky one with dark hair, stepped forward. "Holly, I'm afraid we have to take you in for questioning in the attack on Captain Moran." He glanced apologetically at Travis as he said it.

"The captain was attacked? By who? What happened? Wait, why are you questioning me?" I asked growing alarmed.

Travis's face was a grim mask. "Captain Moran was attacked late Saturday night. He's in the hospital and he says you did it."

"He what? You know I didn't. I was in a car accident. I spent the night hiding in the snow from a maniac." My voice rose at the end and, I'm ashamed to admit, sounded a little hysterical.

The shorter stocky officer who's name badge read Peterson, spoke again. "If you could just show us where you were and we could verify that you were there all night?"

I let out a heavy breath. That old man at the store warned me not to say anything and the valley was clearly hidden. How could I say something without knowing the reason why it had been hidden?

"I'm sorry, I just wandered and I think I hit my head, my memory is not very clear from that night."

Peterson's mouth became a grim line. "Then I'm afraid we'll have to take you in."

"It's okay Holly, I'll take care of everything." Mildred had come up behind me and I jumped when she spoke.

"Thanks Mildred." Officer Peterson went to put the cuffs on when Travis stopped him.

"That's not necessary. It'll be okay Holly. I'll get to the bottom of this."

I looked into his intense blue eyes for a reassurance I wasn't feeling at the moment. Whatever Bonnie and Moran had cooked up, I would beat it. "Of course. I'll come along, just let me get my coat."

I could feel the eyes of the ladies looking at me through the window without even turning around. The ginger haired cop, whose name I didn't catch, held open the back door for me and helped me inside. Oddly enough, when I looked up at my house, Ginger and Friendly were in the window watching me. Did they know what was going on? I knew Mildred would take good care of them and hopefully this misunderstanding would be cleared up soon.

Bonnie

My phone buzzed in my pocket as we were driving the short distance into town and I pulled it out to see a message from an unidentified number but I knew who it was.

"Now you know how it feels." My chest constricted.

It was Bonnie, it couldn't be anyone else. My heart thumped loudly in my chest. I'd never been arrested before. On the other hand, I felt a bit relieved that the shoe had finally dropped. Was this the best Bonnie could do? Moran wasn't even dead. Even if I was found guilty of this crime, which I didn't do, at most it would be community service. But why the birthday ruse?

Another thought hit me then; unless they paid off a judge. Bonnie did have quite a bit of money.

At the station, they led me into a small back room with a table and two chairs. I sat in one facing Detective David Martin. It was at this point I became grateful for my years of dealing with difficult clients, which helped to keep me calm. I hadn't been in a police station since my husband died and certainly not on this side of the table.

"Hi Holly, I'm sorry for this. Travis can't be in here because of the personal conflict but he'll be listening. I need you to tell me what happened Saturday night."

I related the incident with the crash and the person coming after me with a baseball bat. I omitted the whole valley adventure but included my pets coming to rescue me.

"So that's how you survived the freezing temperatures? Your dog and cat?"

"Yes."

He bit the inside of his cheek as he thought.

"Can I ask what happened to Captain Moran?"

Martin took a deep breath and thought for a few moments before answering. "It might be better if you don't know, but someone hit him over the head as he was getting into his car. A woman found him and called 911.

"Bonnie," I breathed and he narrowed his eyes at me.

"I can't say who it was," he said, but there was a slight nod of his head. So, this whole thing was a set up to make me fail. We were interrupted by a knock at the door. Peterson poked his head in, "Mrs. Holcraft's attorney is here."

My what? My eyebrows rose. I didn't have an attorney, maybe Travis got me one. Martin left the room and Theodore Marlowe, probate attorney, entered the room. He was tall, thin and slightly balding and I was ecstatic and slightly confused to see him.

"Well Mrs. Holcraft, it seems as if you've gotten yourself into a bit of a pickle."

"Yes, I suppose so. Don't get me wrong, I'm glad you're here but I thought you were a probate attorney?"

He gave me a hearty chuckle. "I was a prosecuting attorney before I 'retired' to the probate world. Alma gave me a call. They haven't actually filed any charges so you are currently free to go. My advice is not to speak to anyone. Go home, have a good night's rest and see me first thing in the morning."

I breathed a huge sigh of relief and jumped up to give him a hug. "Thank you and I most certainly will. Thank you, thank you, thank you."

"You should actually thank Alma for this."

"Oh, I will. Oh my, how am I supposed to get home?"

"I believe there's someone waiting for you in the lobby that will give you a ride."

I knew they had no reason to hold me. This was all just a fear and intimidation tactic by Bonnie. Despite my relief, I hurried to the lobby, my legs feeling like water. The sooner I left the station, the better I would feel.

Both Alma and Travis were waiting for me. "Oh Alma, how can I ever repay you?" I asked.

She just gave me a quick smile, "I think you should probably hurry home. We can talk tomorrow in a more private setting."

"Of course."

"I believe Detective Smart here is offering you a ride home." She turned and put her hand on his shoulder. "Thank you Travis."

Travis tried to hide a smile and put his hand through my arm to guide me to the door. I sagged into his side in relief. He didn't say a word until we were safely ensconced in his car and driving away from the station.

"Holly, what's going on?" He asked, concern clear in his voice.

"I don't know. Bonnie's trying to get revenge." I watched his silhouette in the dark car as we drove through town.

"No. not that. Alma called me as soon as Mildred let her know what was going on. Then Marlowe called me. They both cautioned me not to say a word about where you were Saturday night."

"They what?" *How could they know?* I'd only told Travis and Vana.

"Here's another weird thing. When I went back to look at your car, all of your tracks, the dog's, the cat's, were gone. It didn't snow that night. I should have been able to follow them but someone made them disappear."

"What? Why didn't you tell me?"

"You were already so upset, I didn't want to worry you further."

I sank back into the car seat, staring straight ahead through the windshield. Someone tried to kill me and then someone erased the tracks. Was it the same person? That didn't make any sense. Why did Alma get me an attorney? Why would they warn Travis not to talk? Was it about the valley? What were they hiding? Alma did act weird when I told her we were using the Blume house. Did it have something to do with the house?

How could the Blume house and the hidden valley be connected? Did it have something to do with the Christmas thefts? Why would Christmas decorations be split up? Blume house had a huge attic, there was plenty of room to store them and if you didn't want to store them there, then why leave a note explaining it?

I was beginning to get a headache. "Maybe we'll get some answers tomorrow," I said. "Will you go to the attorney's office with me?"

Travis glanced my way, "of course I will. I want answers as much as you do."

Was he reading my mind? At my look of surprise he laughed. "Holly, I can read you like a book. I'm not sure what you're thinking but I know you have a ton of questions." He pulled the car to a stop and I was shocked to see that we had arrived at my house. Mildred must have been watching through the window for us, because she opened the door as soon as Travis stopped the car.

"Now get inside and try to sleep." The light on the garage illuminated his face through the windshield showing his warm smile. A smile meant just for me and that warmed my heart.

"I will. Thank you for being here for me. It means a lot."

"I will always be here for you, Holly. Now go. I'll pick you up at 9 am tomorrow."

Later as I lay in bed, one thought kept running through my mind. *What did Mildred know?*

Arguments

W hen I woke in the morning, Mildred was already gone, almost as if she knew I was going to ask her questions. After a shower and a cup of coffee and a few snuggles with Ginger and Friendly, I was feeling a million times better.

I waited for Travis with anticipation, today I was going to get some answers. A knock at the door made me jump. I guess I'm not as relaxed as I thought. With a pleased smile, I hurried to open the door for Travis.

"It's about time," complained Maggs. "It's freezing out here." She barged past me into the house followed closely by Gloria.

"Um, what are you guys doing here?"

"I found them," declared Gloria victoriously.

"You what?" I was thrown completely off balance by their appearance this morning. I glanced at the clock on the wall. It was already after nine and Travis was nowhere around.

"I found all the pieces for the nativity and the Santa and the reindeer."

"Only eight," grunted Maggs.

"There are only eight," muttered Gloria back to her.

"Ladies. Please just explain how you found them." I was not in the mood for this bickering. I was beginning to understand how Mildred felt with the twins.

"It was the twins. Bettie and Dottie," stated Maggs.

Gloria's face looked like a ray of sunshine was shining down on it from the heavens above. She was positively beaming. "They are a whiz at find things on the computer."

"When you can get them to quit bickering," pointed out Maggs, which I considered to be a rather ironic statement coming from her.

"We are going to pick them all up today and we thought you might want to be there when we set them up," explained Gloria.

"Um, sure," I replied hesitantly as I glanced out the front window again.

"Are you looking for Travis?" Asked Gloria. "Captain Moran sent him to Morecroft this morning."

"How do you know that?" I inquired.

"Joanne at the station called me this morning. She told me all about your lawyer springing you from the joint. Oh yeah, I'm supposed to tell you that he won't be coming this morning and your appointment with the lawyer has been rescheduled til Thursday."

Just great. Once again no answers. "You could have at least led with that!" I retorted with frustration.

"Sorry." Gloria shrugged and then the smile was back on her face. "I was just so excited about my news. I got the kids from the high school football team to come over and clean out a space in the front yard for the display. Did you know, there's a concrete pad there? Oh, it's going to be so awesome!"

Maggs rolled her eyes. "Come on loopy, let's get out of here and pick up some reindeer. Eight. Maybe Wendy has a Rudolph."

I rubbed my neck as I watched them leave still bickering about the correct number of reindeer.

"He was only there for just the one foggy night," I heard Gloria argue as I shut the door behind them.

Not one to take anyone's word for anything, I tried calling both Alma and Mr. Marlow but received no answer. I left a message just in case because I hate when callers don't leave messages.

Then I made myself a cup of coffee and sat at the bar with a piece of paper and a pen and wrote down all my questions, dividing the paper into three sections: Hidden Valley, Laurie's death, and Christmas thefts, hoping that something would come to mind.

Under Hidden Valley I had:

- What do Alma and Theodore know, if anything?
- What was that old man talking about?
- What is that rock and how did he know where it was from?
- What secrets?
- Why is the valley walled off?
- Who erased the tracks? Why?

Under Laurie's death was:

- She didn't like the cold but she was dressed for it.
- Why was she outside?
- Did she really slip and fall?
- Was her death an accident?
- Who hit Moran? Because it certainly wasn't me.
- Was it the same one who hit Laurie?

Christmas thefts:

- Is it Jacob?
- Why?
- Who dug the hole in Candace's backyard?
- Is there something hidden inside the decorations?

And finally:

How is my dog getting out of the yard?

I wasn't really sure I wanted an answer to that last one. She had saved me several times now and curiosity was battling with wanting to keep her safe. Who knows what kind of trouble she could get into, not to mention getting hurt. Plus, she brought the cat with her!

These questions were not getting me anywhere. I needed to get to work. I had inspections to schedule on Tom's place and follow ups on all the homes for the Christmas Tour. Evidently now, I also needed to thwart Bonnie's attempts at sabotage again.

Talk about narcissistic, she ruined multiple families lives and blamed it on everyone else but herself and she was still at it.

Caught

O
n Thursday, I staked out Jacob's house. Curiously he had a Santa and reindeer set up in his front yard. The reindeer looked newish but the Santa was old and faded.

I waited until he left, then snuck onto his property. A small shed sat on the back of his property tucked away in the trees. The door was locked but a window on the side didn't close properly and I managed to jimmy it open and climb inside.

Climbing may be exaggerating a bit, mostly I fell through and landed on the dirty floor in a heap. It was dark inside, so I risked turning on my phone flashlight. The shelves were mostly empty except for a large box.

I risked a peek out the window and the rifled through the box. Inside were carefully wrapped figurines of baby Jesus in a manger. I looked closely at one under my light turning it over carefully in my hand. Nothing of any special significance stood out. The features on the face looked old, not like a modern baby would.

"What are you doing in here?" My heart jumped into my throat and I fumbled the figurine I was holding. Fortunately, I only dropped my phone, the light shining up and illuminating the inside of the shed roof.

Jacob was framed in the doorway, a dark shadow against the bright sun outside the outline of a shovel clear in his hand. How had I not heard him unlock the door?

"Are you stealing Santas?" I swallowed a lump in my throat and blurted out, "I found your stash of baby Jesus's."

"Looks like you're the one stealing," he said. If I was about to die, then I certainly wanted some answers first.

"Your Santa, is that the one from Carol's old house?" I couldn't see his face clearly but I could tell by the stiffness in his outline that I had guessed accurately. He backed up away from the door and I stepped forward. He had sat down on a bench by the shed and leaned the shovel next to him.

"How did you guess?" His demeanor seemed resigned.

"I'm not stupid. Your Santa clearly doesn't go with the reindeer. All the Santas you destroyed in the storage shed were new. I don't get it though, why the baby Jesus? What could be hidden in it?"

"Nothing," he said bitterly. "There was nothing in any of them."

"They why steal them?"

"It was my uncle. I didn't want to do it but he's been pressuring me. He said there was a treasure hidden in Appleby. He told me to steal the Santa's and the baby Jesus's."

"Why wouldn't you just tell him no?"

He suddenly became agitated and began pacing up and down. "I couldn't I had no choice!"

"Everyone has a choice, Jacob."

"You don't understand. I lost my job, I was going to lose my house. Every penny I have is tied up in it. He said he wouldn't help me if I didn't do this."

"What do you know about Laurie Culpepper?"

"Who?" He looked thoroughly confused by the question.

"I don't suppose you hit Captain Moran over the head?" His eyes got big and I shook my head. "Never mind. Tell me about this treasure?"

He sat back down and put his head in his hands. "If I tell you everything, will you help me? I know you're really smart."

I opened and closed my mouth a few times and then huffed out a breath. "Sure Jacob. I'll help you. Just tell me what you know."

It was my great grandfather. He was a puzzle master and he used to design crossword puzzles for the newspaper. He designed the clues so that the treasure could be found again one day if the town needed it."

He ran his hands through his hair making it stick up in all directions. "You'll help me right? If my uncle finds out I talked to you, he'll kill me."

I considered him sitting there. His words sounded like truth. "Was there anything in the Santa?"

He kicked at a rock on the ground before answering. "No."

"Do you know what the treasure is or why they hid it?"

He took a long deep breath and let it out slowly. "About a hundred years ago, something happened. A huge treasure was found but the town leaders didn't want it to destroy the town, so they hid it. The secret was passed down through the generations, father to son, you get the idea."

"But you said your uncle told you about it, not your father."

Jacob hung his head. "My dad disappeared when I was a kid, he never had a chance to tell me. My uncle said he ran away but I don't believe it. He loved me. He would never have left me."

"Why didn't your uncle look for it himself?"

Jacob rose suddenly and I jumped back. His face was twisted with anger. "He's the black sheep in the family. No one would trust him with the information but he found out somehow. Will you help me find it?" He looked at me hopefully.

I stared at him in shock. "I said I would help you but I don't know how I can find a hundred year old treasure."

"She said you were smart," he said almost accusingly.

"Who did?"

"My uncle's girlfriend. She said you were too smart for your own good." His eyes were bloodshot and there were dark circles beneath from lack of sleep. He looked tired and defeated.

The mom in me rose to the surface and I gave his shoulder a quick squeeze. "Jacob, I will do my very best to help you. Of course, you have to promise not to steal anymore decorations. Promise?"

He nodded his head weakly. "I promise."

"I've got to go now, okay?" I was almost to the front of the house when I stopped and called back. "Just one more thing Jacob. Who is your uncle?" My phone buzzed in my pocket and by the time I looked back up, Jacob was gone.

Blume House

Vana drove me through town with Chloe and Ginger to survey the Christmas decorations and ensure everything was ready to go for the tour tomorrow night. It had snowed this afternoon and all the pine trees looked fuzzy on their branches. Most everyone in town celebrated with lights during this time of the year and everywhere looked festive against the backdrop of snow.

As we circled the lake, a white mist rose from off the water. Ice skaters wearing light up necklaces made the rounds on the rink. Most of the businesses were decorated and Christmas music could be heard through the closed doors.

Completing the circle, I headed my car up the hill to the Blume house. I parked and Chloe, Ginger and I made our way across the lawn to join the other volunteers who were standing about admiring the decorations.

We'd done it. The life-size nativity scene was complete on the front lawn. Baby Jesus in the manger was safely ensconced within the manger while Mary and Joseph kept watch under a beautiful wooden stable. Sheep and donkeys kept watch, along with one very large doberman shepherd. Ginger was never one to be left out.

Santa and the reindeer pranced upon the opposite of the snow covered lawn. Okay, pranced is a relative term as they are plastic and stationary, but if they could have pranced, they would.

The Christmas tree shone with a thousand twinkling lights and the piece de resistance, a giant lit star, crowned the top of the tree.

"I found another star." Chloe held a medium sized star up to me. "I think it goes above baby Jesus." The crystal star was exquisite. Handling it with care, I walked over and surveyed the nativity scene. Sure enough, there was a little hook for the star to hang just at the peak of the stable.

I hung the star and plugged it into the extension cord running down the back of the nativity. Whoever had designed this decades ago had done an excellent job of running electrical lines through out the stable so all the characters could be illuminated.

I stepped back to admire the scene and the nativity scene went dark. Thankfully, we were testing the display in advance of the tour to ensure everything worked. There's nothing worse than setting everything up and discovering a string of lights doesn't work. Everything we installed was tested multiple times during the decorating process to ensure there were no loose wires or lights.

"Don't worry Chloe, I'll fix it." I followed the extension cord back around the house to where it was plugged in and wiggled it till the lights came on, then took a shortcut through the house to view the scene from the broad living room windows.

Gasping, I stopped and stared at the mantle in the living room. A smaller nativity had been installed on the mantle above the fireplace. The light from Rudolph's nose was shining through the window and lighting up the star of this little manger.

That's not what made me gasp though. One of the bricks was glowing. Dragging a chair over, I climbed up to take a closer look. The brick wasn't loose. Jiggling it did nothing so I pushed on it and heard a click across the room.

The windows of the old manor house were separated by wood paneling and one of these panels now stood open. I climbed down from the chair and crossed the room to the open panel.

"Holly! Are you in here?" Vana's voice rang out from the direction of the kitchen and the lights promptly shut off. A chill crept over me and I pressed the panel closed behind my back as she entered the room.

"Yes. I was just going to view the display through the front windows and then the lights went out again." Just then the lights popped back on. *Was it Dorothy?* Dorothy Blume was the maid for the owners' of the house in the 1800's and when they passed away, the house was left to Dorothy who maintained it with meticulous care. And sometimes, things unexplainable happened in this house.

If it hadn't been for the lights, I would have told Lucy about the panel, now I would have to return later and find out by myself. I certainly don't believe in ghosts but why take any chances?

"Oh, it does look magnificent. Everyone did an excellent job." The lights from the display illuminated Vana's face. "Why are you frowning?" she asked.

I raised my eyebrows at the unexpected question. "Was I?" Of course I was because I was wondering why Rudolph's nose was no longer shining on the nativity star on the fireplace. "I'm just going through everything that still needs to be done in my head. At least I can tick this one off my list. Although, perhaps we should get a generator just in case."

Vana had returned to admiring the display. "Probably a good idea." The lights shown brightly in the darkness, illuminating the faces of the small group of volunteers outside.

"Hey, why is Rudolph out there?" I asked, counting out nine reindeer in front of Santa's sleigh. "Uh, oh."

Maggs and Gloria each had a hold of Rudolph and were arguing over his position. "I should probably get out there," I said, my feet still planted firmly on the floor.

"Do they do this all the time?" asked Vana, mesmerized by the scene playing out before her.

"Yup." The other volunteers were now gravitating over toward the twosome. The house lights flickered suddenly. "Yeah, yeah, I'm going."

"It's not right that Rudolph only gets just the one night," argued Maggs. "He was so important and then Santa just drops him? I think that puts Santa on the naughty list."

Gloria cocked her head sideways and put her hand on her hip. "His light would give out Santa's position immediately. He was a security risk."

"She is right," said Patty timidly.

Maggs threw her hands in the air. "I thought you were on my side?"

"Ladies!" I called from the porch steps. "I'm sure Santa loves all his reindeer equally."

"Hmph, I don't think that's true," muttered Maggs.

"Nonetheless, I'm sure that Rudolph can be a part of our celebration as he's not flying. None of the reindeer *here* will be flying anytime soon." I thrust my forefinger in the air as Gloria opened her mouth to speak. "We can let Rudolph stay and there will be nine reindeer this year." Especially since I think he's going to help me solve a mystery.

Maggs drew in a deep breath and straightened her shoulders as she gave Gloria a triumphant smirk.

"Now let's clean up so we can all get home."

Gloria marched straight over to me. "You know, there's going to be no living with her after this?"

"Under every cloud a little rain must fall," said Cindy in commiseration.

"Huh?" we all turned to look at her.

"I don't think that's how that goes," said Vana. "But it does make sense."

"It's 'into each life some rain must fall' by Henry Wadsworth Longfellow," said Maggs proudly, evidently still riding her high of winning.

"And so it starts," muttered Gloria.

156

"Okay, great! I'm shutting off the lights and locking the doors in exactly five minutes," I declared to forestall any more arguing. This of course, sent everyone scurrying to grab their belongings and get to their vehicles.

I cast one last longing look at the house before climbing into Vana's car with Ginger and shutting the door. She cranked up the heat as she drove down the hill. "Everything appears to be coming together nicely."

"Uh huh," I said, as I watched the house fading from sight in the rear view mirror.

"What are you doing?"

"One more sec," I said instead of answering. "Okay. I was waiting until we were out of view of the house."

"Because...?"

"I found something in there and I don't think Dorothy knows that you know about the valley."

"Say what? Who's Dorothy?"

I looked at her and thought back to the Fall Festival. "Oh, that's right, you weren't a volunteer then. I proceeded to tell her about Dorothy and how I thought the house tripped Meredith as she tried to escape down the stairs and then wouldn't let Carol out of the front door.

Vana's eyes got bigger as I spoke. "You think that Dorothy Blume, the maid, haunts Blume house and you don't want to get her mad at you. Do I have that right?"

I huffed and sat back in my seat. "When you put it like that, I sound crazy, but yes. That's it in a nutshell."

Vana mouthed the word 'wow.'

"It's just, what if it is haunted? I don't really want a ghost mad at me. Would you?" I gave her a sheepish smile.

"Ghosts aside." I swear she rolled her eyes at me. "What do you think is in that compartment?"

"I don't know. Something to do with the hidden valley though. Too many people were involved in this secret and it was kept for such a long time."

Did Laurie know the secret? Is that why she was killed? Who knocked out Moran? What was the connection?

Frustration

The old man at the gas station knew something and I had to find him, so early the next morning, I called an Uber.

After a cursory hello and where are you going, the young driver lapsed into silence which suited me just fine. I sat in the back seat and leaned my head against the window, oblivious to the view outside.

Did the hidden valley have anything to do with Jacob's secret treasure? Something about the old guy scared me and I hoped there would be other customers there, which is why I was going now, in the middle of the day.

As the driver pulled into the station, I asked him to wait. Unlike the driver at the beach, this driver agreed quickly. Business must be slow out here. With my hand on the handle of the door to the store I hesitated and peered through the window inside,

"What do you want?" barked a gruff voice behind me. I shrieked and whirled around. My stomach took a few more seconds to return to its rightful place. The old man stood behind me holding an empty trash can.

I opened my mouth to speak, gulped and then began again.

"Hi sir, actually I came here to speak to you."

"What for?" He leaned closer, his brows drawn together with suspicion.

"I, um, I was here the other day," I began nervously, "with a rock."

He immediately looked around and then, grabbing my arm, drug me around the corner of the building. "I told you not to talk about that.

"I haven't," I said, suddenly deciding to bluff. "But I know about it and the hidden treasure."

Oddly he looked almost hopeful. "How did you find out?" No, never mind. It doesn't matter. It'll be all over now. The town will be destroyed. it will all have been for nothing."

"No...I'm sorry, what is your name?"

He signed looking deflated. "It's Peter, Peter Martin." A tear traveled slowly down his cheek. Now I felt appalled. I made an old man cry. I put my hand reassuringly on his arm.

"It's okay Peter, I'm the only one that knows."

This did not console him. "But if you found it, others will too. I read they're having a party at the Blume house with the original decorations."

Things began to click in my brain. The secret in the wall. I had to find out what it was.

"Maybe not. Why don't you tell me your side and Maybe we can figure out how to keep the secret."

Peter's attitude instantly changed. "I can't. My brother tried to kill me for this secret. I'll take it to my grave. Now git, leave!"

Frustrated, I backed away and jumped in the car to get away for the second time.

Somehow I had to sneak into Blume house and find what was hidden in the wall.

Tour

The rest of the day I was kept busy running around all day with last minute issues. Jo still hadn't gotten back to me with the results from the rock. I didn't have a chance to look for the compartment until the tour was already underway.

I hurried to the Blume house under the excuse that I was going to open it up. My hand trembled as I tried to insert the key into the lock. Feeling relief at the lock clicking open, I slipped inside. I had only mere moments before someone else showed up.

Dragging a chair from the dining room to the fireplace, I pressed on the brick, letting out the breath I hadn't realized I'd been holding as I heard the slight click behind me.

Now was the moment of truth. Taking a deep breath, I let it out slowly to steady myself and reached into the dark space behind the panel.

I nearly shrieked when my hand touched something soft. Rats came suddenly to mind until I realized it was a piece of woven fabric. Unless rats had taken up weaving, this wasn't one.

I pulled it carefully out and then stashed it in my purse as I heard a car pull into the drive and headlights flashed across the room. There was just enough time to close the panel and put the chair back before the front door opened.

This was so frustrating. All I wanted to do was take a look in the bag.

A hundred year old secret and it was *right there* and I couldn't take a look. Instead, I smiled at the newcomers and welcomed them into the house.

More cars were pulling in. The tour was only open to the ground floor of the house so I snuck upstairs.

Finally! Now was my chance to see what the mysterious papers were. I hurried to the second bedroom. The door creaked as I opened it and again when I shut the door behind me. At least I'll know if someone comes in.

I pulled the bag out of my purse, huh, the cloth was remarkably undusty. Undoing the tie at the top of the bag, I carefully removed the pages inside using the light coming in the window to read the papers. The first one was a map with the valley clearly marked and the second was a deed that conveyed the land to Phillip Harding, the old guy I called that said he didn't know anything.

"What's that you've got there Holly?" I shrieked and spun around on the spot. Travis was standing just inside the door.

"How, how did you get in here?"

"I opened the door," he said as if I was two.

"I mean without it creaking?" I walked past the puzzled man to open the door myself and show him and that darn door didn't make a sound. Now I was just annoyed. "I don't know if I should say in here," I said as I glanced at the ceiling.

Travis's eyes followed mine around the room.

"Are you looking for a ghost?" he asked.

"Maybe. Fine, it's a map and a deed." I showed him the papers, once again glancing around nervously.

"Wow, Henry never said anything about this."

"Henry?"

"My wife's uncle. Her family lived here since the early 1900s. He moved away a few years ago."

"I'm sorry, who's Henry and what does he have to do with Phillip Harding?"

"They were cousins. Their families lived next door to each other. Henry's retired and living in Florida. I heard Phillip moved there himself several years ago. It was my understanding they had sold all their property here when they moved. Is this the hidden valley?"

"I think it must be."

In the silence that followed the door creaked open and I jumped. I dashed out the door and down the stairs but no one was there. I walked slowly back up the stairs.

"Dorothy wants us to go," I said, taking the papers from Travis and returning them to my purse.

"You know you still owe me a lunch," he said.

"I do," That tingly feeling swept through my belly again as I said the words.

"How about Monday?" he asked.

Sudden sadness dispelled the tingle. "I can't, it's Laurie's funeral."

"I'm sorry, would you like me to go with you?"

I stopped on the landing and he continued another step before stopping himself.

"What's going on with Moran's accusations against me?"

He stood one step below me bringing us both to eye level. "He has no proof it was you and because he got hit on the back of his head, the district attorney is refusing to prosecute."

A rumble in the step made me continue down the stairs.

Downstairs the party was in full swing. Santa was handing out gifts in front of the fireplace while guests filled plates with cookies. I spied Gloria in the corner of the living room talking animatedly with Maggs. I overheard reindeer and nearly headed the other direction.

"Gloria, the place looks amazing. Who did you get for Santa?" I asked.

Gloria looked around to make sure no kids were nearby then whispered. "Ben Brown. Isn't he great?"

"He certainly is." Through the front window I spotted Alma, Theodore Marlow, the old man from the gas station and an elderly gentleman admiring the nativity scene. Although I don't know that admiring was the correct word. Alma had a pinched look to her face. A hand on my arm caught my attention. It was Jo wearing a figure hugging red dress. "Holly, so good to see you. The tour is amazing this year." She gave me a quick hug and whispered in my ear, "I have your answer," as she handed me a small wrapped gift.

I gave her my thanks and slipped it into my purse.

"Who was that woman?" asked Maggs.

"My assistant Jo."

"But I thought your assistant was male." She cut off abruptly as Mildred elbowed her in the side.

"It's a long story," I said. A glance out the window revealed my group of interest was gone.

"Shouldn't we start the caroling?" asked Cindy.

Gloria and Maggs passed out candles as the patrons filed out the front door. Soon the front lawn was filled with candle light reflecting off the snow.

Someone dimmed the outside lights and the stars blazed above us in the night sky. It was a beautiful evening. Travis came up and wrapped his arms around me. I relaxed against his chest enjoying the moment as the sounds of Silent Night filled the air. I half expected to see Santa fly overhead. He definitely wouldn't be needing Rudolph.

People began to disperse after the songs ended. Tabitha offered to take the remaining food to our local food bank along with the donations we had collected at each house.

We all helped Gloria clean up Blume house. "Hey, I have a thought," yelled Gloria from the kitchen where she was washing dishes. "Can we put things in the wrong places and see if the ghost moves them?

"Do you really want a ghost made at you? I yelled back. Travis came out wiping his hands dry on a towel.

"You don't really believe in ghosts do you?"

"I plead the fifth," I said looking at the ceiling. "Thanks for helping with the dishes."

"Of course dear. I'm just want you to see I'm well-rounded boyfriend material."

"Can't wait to find out what else you can do," I replied, smiling.

Maggs bustled by," You two need to demonstrate your putting away skills so we can get out of here."

"Yes, Maggs," I rolled my eyes and Travis stifled a laugh behind his hand.

"Did any of you see Alma tonight?" I asked.

"I did," piped up Cindy. "She didn't stay long. Why?"

"I feel like she's avoiding me," I said. "I haven't seen her since I was taken in for questioning."

"You should sue them for false arrest," declared Maggs.

"I wasn't arrested," I replied. The lights flickered.

"I think your ghost wants us to hurry up," quipped Maggs.

"Mustn't get the ghost angry," said Travis with a peck on my cheek. The warmth of that kiss carried me through the rest of the evening. It wasn't until the wee hours of the morning that I remembered Jo's present.

Wrap up

My eyes popped open. Ginger was snoring and Friendly was snoozing on my arm. Carefully extricating myself, I slipped from under the covers and padded to the front door to find my purse hanging on the rack beside it.

I turned on an end lamp and settled on the couch in front of the window. Snow was just beginning to fall.

Jo had wrapped the box in red paper tied with a gold ribbon which came untied when I pulled one end. The paper wasn't taped and pulling it off revealed a note written on the inside of the paper. Such a clever girl. The small box contained only my rock, now slightly smaller.

Picking up the paper, I read, "The geologist said this rock contains silver, originally mined in Appleby in the early 1900s. The vein was tapped out and abandoned.

Silver! That had to be it. If that valley was filled with silver, that could be the treasure. As a real estate agent, I had heard horror stories of towns polluted by mining. No wonder they wanted to hide it.

Now I held the secret in my hands. How do I keep the secret? How can I hide what a whole town kept hidden?

I knew someone who had answers and I was going to get them in the morning.

Fortified with several cups of coffee and a few more hours of sleep, I headed out the door. Ginger and Friendly had both eaten and gone back to sleep on my bed. A car pulled up outside and I dashed through the new fallen snow. It gave off a ghostly glow in the early morning light. I had decided to be the early bird that catches the worm.

"And where are we off to so bright and early this morning?" asked Travis.

"I think I know who erased my tracks in the snow and I fully intend to get answers this morning." I gave him the address and a short time later, we pulled into Emmeline's driveway.

At my insistent knocking at six am, Emmeline finally answered the door in her black silk bathrobe.

"Holly, what are you doing here?" A huge yawn cracked her jaws. Mascara from last night left streaks around her eyes. She would regret that when she was older.

"Hello Emmeline, I'm sorry to disturb you so early." I replied as I pushed my way past her. "What room is Alma in, please?"

"Upstairs at the end of the hall."

"Thank you," I said and headed up.

"She's not up yet," she called after me.

"That's what I'm hoping," I muttered under my breath. I heard her offering Travis coffee, which he accepted.

I entered Alma's room without knocking. "Good morning Alma. rise and shine." I flung open the curtains, letting in the early morning light. To her credit, Alma took my rude intrusion with grace, sit up in bed and pulling her eye mask off.

"Holly. I suspected you would find me after Phillip told me about your conversation."

"Phillip Harding?"

"Yes. What do you want to know?" She said with resignation in her voice.

"I know about the valley. Someone tried to kill me and I found it by accident. Peter told you I found the rock didn't he?" Alma gave the briefest of nods.

"You covered my tracks. The tow truck driver told you." It just made sense. Another tiny nod. I would have missed it had I not been watching her.

"How many of you are involved in this?"

"There's only about ten of us left now," she said throwing back the covers. She swung her legs over the side of the bed and then retrieved her robe from a chair against the wall. She put it on and pulled the belt tight.

"Holly, I'm so sorry about the trouble with William. He's been a thorn in our side for more years than I care to remember.

She picked up a picture of a softball team from the bedside table and ran her fingers over it. "William?" I prompted.

"Captain Moran. He's been trying to unearth the secret for years."

Another piece of the puzzle just slid into place. "Moran is Jacob's uncle. Bonnie is his girlfriend."

"Yes." Her one word answer annoyed me.

"Peter said his father disappeared when he was a child, yet he's only been living one town over?" I asked in disbelief.

"No, he came back only a month ago." She looked at me sadly. "His brother tried to kill him to get the answers. He threatened Jacob. Peter knew the only way to save his son was to leave. It's also why he couldn't tell him the secret."

Moran and Bonnie were certainly made for each other. Unfortunately, I only had Jacob and Alma's word. Without evidence, there was nothing to charge them with.

"The nativity didn't really hold the secret did it?"

"This time she smiled. "No. It was a decoy created a long time ago by James Harding, Phillip's great grandfather to keep people from finding the truth. It was Jacob's great grandfather's idea. Send people on a wild goose chase that won't ever be solved. There is no hidden clue to the treasure."

I shook my head at her. "But there is and I found it. I have the deed to the valley. It was hidden at Blume house. Rudolph's nose lit up a brick on the fireplace and when I pushed it, a door popped open in the front window frame.

She looked at me in disbelief. "That's not possible," she said slowly, her face pale. "There's no deed."

I pulled the deed from my purse and gave it to her.

"The nativity really did harbor a secret?" She appeared to be at a loss for words and it suddenly made me angry. A young child was deprived his father over a stupid joke. How different might Jacob's life have been if his father hadn't left. Captain Moran was as corrupt as they come.

"You'll have to ask Dorothy about that," I declared angrily, snatching the deed back, and stomping out the door.

I dashed a quick text off to Mildred as soon as Travis and I were back in the car.

Help

"Ladies, I'm so glad you could all make it." Mildred had followed the instructions in my text and the members of the mystery book club were once again gathered in my living room.

The ladies sat entranced as I told my story. "So what do we do now?" I asked.

"Why don't you have it declared a historical monument?" said Bettie.

At the sudden strange voice, we all jumped.

"Mom? How did you get in here?" I gasped. My mother, Dottie and Bettie were lined up in the hallway.

"Dottie picked the lock to the garage of course. Bettie saw all the cars arriving through her binoculars and of course i knew you were up to no good.

"So you broke into my house?"

"You worked together?" gasped Mildred in awe.

"Honey it's for your own good." said my mom.

I opened my mouth to speak when Cindy intervened. "What was that you said dear, about a historical monument?"

Bettie walked over to the couch, hitched up her skirt a bit and perched on the arm next to Cindy. "You can have the valley declared a historical monument. It's used to preserve a segment of the past. No one will ever be allowed to develop it.

"My sister is a lawyer in land management," called Dottie proudly from the kitchen where she and my mom were sitting at the bar.

"You're supporting each other now?" mumbled Mildred, her mouth agape.

"That's how she knew!" I exclaimed excitedly. "Cindy said they held the old timers breakfast at the Blume house and talked about declaring it a historical monument. That's why she let us find the deed now."

"Who is she? and what are you talking about?" asked my mom.

Speaking slowly as if explaining to a child, I said, "Dorothy. We can have the valley registered as protected lands. No one will ever be able to mine the silver there and ruin the town. That's why they hid it in the first place.

"They didn't want the land contaminated by the chemicals used to extract the silver from the ore. At the very least, that entire valley would have been deforested, not to mention the river that runs through it. Our beautiful valley would have been devastated," I said.

"The valley no one knows about," muttered Maggs.

"They will," I said. "Bettie, you're a lawyer?'

"I was. I don't have a license here," she said regretfully.

A huge smile wreathed my face. "No, but Theodore Marlowe does. Tell me, when does the protection begin?"

"As soon as you file a hold is put on any plans for development. The protection lasts until the application is approved or denied."

I stood up and began pacing while thinking. "So we take a chance that it doesn't get approved and everyone learns of it."

"I still don't know who Dorothy is," complained my mom.

"She's the ghost of the maid who used to own Blume house," Cindy said with a little lift of her shoulders, as if it was the most normal thing in the world.

My mom put her hand over her mouth as she gasped in shock. "Do not tell me you believe in ghosts. I raised you better than that."

I stopped abruptly in front of Gloria who sat back at my sudden appearance.

"Gloria, how did you find the diary with all the names of the people that the nativity and Santa sets went to?" I asked, hoping to prove my point.

"There was a loose floorboard that popped up in the attic when I stepped on it and it was underneath."

Cindy sat nodding her head. "The ghost showed it to her so we could put the display together."

My mom put her hand to her forehead as if she was going to faint, which I sincerely doubted she would do from the height of the bar stool. "I don't believe it. It's an old house. It was going to happen at some point."

"You've got to admit it was brilliant. By splitting up the set, no one would display one piece so unless everyone came together, the display would never be whole," I said, completely ignoring my mother's theatrics. An idea popped into my head and I stopped in front of Gloria once again.

"How on earth did you get all these people to just give up their pieces? They must have been hiding them for generations."

"For most people they were just junk they didn't want anymore but it was in the parents' will that they had to keep it. Some of them had two or three pieces because as families moved away, they left them behind with other families."

That comment shocked me. "I didn't know they knew each other, if it was a secret."

"Oh yes," said Gloria. "They all belong to the old timers group."

"Which brings us back full circle. Alma admitted the nativity had nothing to do with the secret. It was just a misdirection. Except." I paused dramatically at this point. "There was a secret panel in the wall at the Blume house, which opened when I pressed on a brick at the fireplace, which was illuminated by Rudolph's nose shining through the window."

"AHA!" yelled Maggs, with such force that we all jumped. "I knew Rudolph was vitally important to the story." She leaned back in her chair with her arms crossed on her chest and a self-satisfied smile on her face.

"Hmph," was all Gloria could think of to say.

"What did you find in the wall, dear?" asked Mildred, redirecting our attention back to the story at hand.

"It's a deed, which I'm pretty sure is for the hidden valley, conveying it to Phillip Harding. I saw him at the Blume house during the tour, meeting with Alma," I said.

"Phillip Harding?" said Mildred. "Why he's descended from the original settlers of this town in the 1800s. He only moved away several years ago because his body couldn't handle the cold anymore. He retired to Florida. He family used to live in Carol Oates's old place. They owned a lot of property around here."

I looked at her astounded.

"What?" she said. "I own a store, people talk."

"Great. Bettie, if I give you Marlowe's number, will you walk him through the steps to handle this? We're also going to need to have him contact Phillip Harding and have him agree to this protection."

With everything settled, everyone left for home to get ready for the sad task of attending Laurie's funeral tomorrow.

Revelation

The morning sky was overcast and snow began gently falling by the time I approached the funeral home.

Laurie's funeral was a sad affair. The open casket was situated at the front of the funeral hall with chairs set up in rows in front of it for the guests. Flowers were set up in displays on either side of the casket.

Photos from her life were lined up at the back of the hall. One frame I recognized from Alma's bedside table so I took a closer look. It was a girls softball team, the Morecroft Eagles.

"That's how we first met," said Tabitha. "We were on the same team. Caroline too, although she'll never admit it now. And Emmeline's mother."

The other photos showed Laurie as a child and at various business functions. "Where did you get all the photos," I asked Mildred.

"Her son sent them. I didn't know he kept so many and some I got from her house and her friends brought a few."

"We should probably pay our respects," I said. "The service is going to start soon."

Looking at dead bodies is not my thing, but I felt I had to. She had been a fellow real estate agent and a member of my Christmas committee. It wouldn't be right not to.

She looked beautiful in her lovely blue dress and the jewelry complemented it nicely, although it was all wrong. Glancing around the room, I saw Patty seated in the back row.

"Hi Patty," I whispered as I took a seat next to her.

"She looks so peaceful," commented Patty.

"Yes, she does," I agreed. "I wonder if I could take a look at the pictures you took of her at the Christmas party?"

"Sure." She pulled out her phone and flipped through the photos, stopping when she reached the ones of Laurie.

I took the phone and slowly scrolled through them until I found the one I wanted and then zoomed in.

"What are you looking for?" she asked curiously.

Holding the phone in her direction I showed her what I had found. "She's not wearing the same jewelry. Mildred told me she was going to have her in the same outfit."

A hand on my shoulder made me jump. People really needed to stop sneaking up on me. I need to grow another pair of eyes in the back of my head like in that Outer Limits show.

"Sorry, I heard my name," hissed Mildred. "What are you looking at?"

I pointed at the jewelry. "Oh, yes. Well someone broke in and stole her jewelry so I put mine on her. Dan assured me he would have it back to me after the service."

I looked at her dumbfounded. "Someone stole a dead woman's cheap jewelry?"

"Mmhm," Mildred nodded. "Maybe they didn't know." That unsettled feeling began rattling around in my head again. I was missing something important.

The Reverend began the service and I was left alone with my thoughts. He had known Laurie well and regaled us with funny stories of her through the years. I frowned as Caroline stepped to the front to speak.

"I really didn't know Laurie but she was assigned to my house and was doing an excellent job before this terrible accident. It is so wonderful to see that she was beloved by so many of her family and friends."

And suddenly it all clicked into place. Laurie had been murdered. I had no proof, but I was pretty sure where to find it.

I watched as Caroline slipped out to the foyer of the funeral home and I left my seat to follow her. Jackets and boots lined the walls of the empty foyer. Where had she gone? I approached the door to check outside and she stepped from behind the open door as I walked through.

I turned to find her holding a gun in her hand. She twitched the barrel of the gun toward the door. "Let's take a drive shall we?" she whispered.

I reached for my coat. "Leave it," she hissed. The air outside was bitterly cold as I stepped through the door and slipped in the fresh snow. Caroline had me drive her car and we headed toward the estates.

"What's going on Caroline," I asked. deliberately pronouncing her name the wrong way.

"Don't play stupid Holly. I know you figured it out. I saw you looking at the softball photo."

"Actually that wasn't it," I said. "It was the jewelry and now I know it was you that tried to kill me leaving the estates."

"You should have left it alone. I warned you in that note on your car, but did you listen? Nooo," she snarled.

"I don't understand why you tried to kill me."

"Because you were investigating Laurie's death."

"Except, I wasn't. It was the perfect crime," I replied.

"Don't lie. Bonnie said you were investigating."

And there it was. Another answer dropped into place. If Caroline killed me then Bonnie's hands would be clean. "Tell me Caroline, did you really kill Laurie because you wear cheap jewelry?"

"I have a reputation to uphold. What would people think if they knew that woman had the same jewelry as me." she said haughtily. "And now you'll just be another poor soul frozen in the snow. She directed me to park just the other side of the tunnel to the estates. "Get out."

I couldn't die here. People would find the gate. Snow was falling steadily and the road up the hill had at least three inches of snow covering it. I had to delay and hope someone would come by.

"How long have you been working with Bonnie?"

"I'm not working with Bonnie," she scoffed. the gun never wavering. "Now get out. Don't make me say it again."

My hand slipped on the door handle and hit a large flashlight lying on the floor next to the seat. Opening the door, I made sure to slip on the snow when exiting the car. I clutched the door to remain upright.

Caroline rounded the front of the car and came toward me. I could stand here frozen and die for sure or take a chance.

"Bonnie wants you to kill me so you take the fall. Travis is looking into Laurie's death, it's only a matter of time before he finds you."

"Ha! I know you amateur sleuths are always keeping everything secret until the big reveal. There's not going to be any big reveal for you."

In anger, she waved the gun towards the opposite side of the street and in one motion, I threw the heavy flashlight at her and then tackled her.

Her feet slipped and her head collided with the side of the car. She collapsed in the snow. The sound of sleigh bells filled the air and relief flooded through me as a horse drawn carriage came around the corner carrying Ben and the twins, Maggs, Tabitha and another gentleman all bundled up in blankets.

The pulled up alongside me and Ben hopped to the ground where he promptly secured Caroline's gun while Dottie called 911.

Maggs stood over her holding a giant candy cane like a club.

"What are you doing here?" I asked in amazement.

Bettie piped up first. "Your mom wanted to go to the funeral."

"Of someone she didn't know?" I asked puzzled.

"When we got to the funeral home," continued Bettie, "you were gone. Maggs said you were following Caroline. Dottie saw the photo of her playing baseball. Well, I put that together with the attack on you and figured out she was up to no good."

"How did you know about the attack?" Once again bewildered at the amount of information my mom had managed to attain in the one short week she had been here.

"Joanne told her," popped up Dottie, holding her hand over the receiver of the phone.

"My mom knows Joanne?" I managed to squeak out.

"It's a good thing to or we wouldn't have found you in time."

"And Ben?"

"He promised us a sleigh ride and the snow was getting heavy. So it just made sense," continued Bettie.

Caroline groaned at my feet and Maggs waved the candy cane at her face.

"Maggs, stop please. The police will be here soon," I pleaded.

"Oh let her do it," yelled Tabitha. "She deserves it for killing our friend."

Fortunately, we all heard the sound of police sirens and Maggs reluctantly backed off.

"Where is my mom?" I asked, but I needn't have because as the first car pulled to a stop, she jumped out of the front passenger seat.

"Thank you Travis dear. Oh honey are you okay?" she asked giving me a quick look over then turned to Dottie and Bettie, hugging them and giving them air kisses.

"Oh, thank you wonderful ladies for saving my baby girl. And you too dear Ben." This last comment was accompanied by sultry glance and a quick wink. I rolled my eyes.

"I guess we're just chopped liver," grumped Maggs to Tabitha.

"Holly, are you alright?" Now that voice sent warm flutterings all through me. Travis placed a blanket around my shoulders and pulled me tight.

"I am now," I murmured. Two officers handcuffed Caroline and sat her in the back of the patrol car.

A loud obnoxious voice cut through the air. "Now, now, what's going on here? Why isn't this woman behind bars?" Captain Moran's jacket looked like he'd slept in it. Several times.

"Ah, Captain Moran. Caroline here was just telling us how she hit you over the head when she went to steal Laurie's jewelry from Dr. Whitby's house." She hadn't, it was mostly a guess, but it made sense. Moran's face went pale in the weak afternoon light.

Travis blocked his path. "You knew that didn't you?"

The two men glared at each other. "I have no idea what you're talking about," smirked Moran.

It was then I realized I hadn't told Travis about Jacob and Moran being behind the Christmas thefts. Caroline began screaming about a lawyer from the patrol car. That's when Jacob showed up.

"Hey uncle." he said in greeting. "Holly and I have been talking." Moran's eyes grew wide. It was at this point the man in the carriage stood up. "Jacob?" he called hesitantly.

Jacob squinted at the man for a moment then said, "Dad?" in a weak voice. I watched in wonder as Peter from the convenience store stepped down from the carriage and Jacob rushed into his arms.

"I'm never going to leave you again," he cried. I looked away to see Moran's car driving away in the distance.

All's well

I ran into Dixie in town at the shops the next day. She looked really great and happy. Tall and thin like her mother, with blonde hair and hazel eyes, she could have anybody she wanted, so why she stayed with Toby was beyond me.

"You look like you're doing well, " I said.

"I am, I really am," she replied. "I heard my mom ruined your date."

"She did," I said. "But Travis was really an angel about it."

"You really should keep a guy like him, Holly."

"Dixie," I began hesitantly. "About Toby."

"He's changed Holly. He's been in rehab for the last two years. I didn't tell mom because she's always so snoopy."

I couldn't deny that. Shelby was very snoopy. Of course, it probably had to do with her job as well as being a mother. "Can I buy you a cup of coffee at Mildred's?"

"I would love that." She smiled and her whole face lit up.

The bell over the door tinkled as we entered Mildred's candy shop. Cindy saw me and ran over excitedly waving a paper over her head. "Bettie did it," she yelled excitedly. "Bettie got the historical designation."

I looked around and realized Dottie, Bettie, my mom, Mildred, Alma, Theodore Marlowe, Maggs and Gloria were all in the shop, apparently celebrating. "How did you get it so fast?" I asked.

Alma stood up. "Theodore had the judge call an emergency session of the town council last night and they took a vote. Phillip signed over the deed to the property to the town. It's now a refuge for the wildlife and will never be open to the public."

I frowned as I saw only one problem with this. "What about Moran?"

The door tinkled behind me. "He's been fired," stated Travis. I looked back at Alma who nodded.

"I believe both he and Bonnie have left the area," added Alma.

Relief battled with doubt inside of me. Did this mean her revenge was over or did it mean I now had two enemies to contend with?

Author Notes

Christmas is only three months away and I'm already busy getting Christmas gifts together. My husband and I just celebrated eighteen years since our first date at the end of August. We went to see one of the Jason Bourne movies and I felt sick and asked to be taken home. He thought I didn't like him but showed up the next day with flowers to take me to the annual fair. We've been together ever since. Not the fair, no. It got cut down from two weeks to one and then split with the animal auction in one month and the fair rides and concerts moved to another month. I guess you could say our relationship is definitely doing better than the poor fair.

We will also be welcoming two new grandsons in October and January. That will make sixteen for us.

It was December of last year when I decided to write a Christmas story for Holly and her friends and now it's done! Next up, Holly and her friends decide to have an open house at a remote cabin in the mountains. Let's be honest, it's probably not their greatest idea, especially when a gunman on the run shows up. What could he possibly be searching for in the mountains during winter?

While you're waiting for the next book to come out, trying making two of my favorite cookies on the next page.

WHAT'S NEXT?

Sign up for my newsletter at <u>subscribepage.io/J9FVtd</u> and be the first to be notified when my next story is published.

You can check out all my books at MRDollschniederAuthor.com

Recipes

MAGIC COOKIE BARS

I absolutely love the chewiness of these bars. They are not particularly a family favorite but they are a me favorite.

- 1 ½ cups graham cracker crumbs
- ½ cup butter, melted
- 1 (14 ounce) can Sweetened Condensed Milk
- 2 cups semisweet chocolate morsels
- 1 ⅓ cups flaked coconut
- 1 cup chopped nuts

Directions

- Preheat the oven to 350 degrees F (175 degrees C). If using a glass dish, preheat the oven to 325 degrees F (165 degrees C). Coat a 9x13-inch baking dish with cooking spray.
- To make the graham cracker crumbs, place the crackers in a plastic freezer bag and then use a rolling pin to grind them into crumbs. This works really well. You may have to do the crackers in batches.
- Mix graham cracker crumbs and butter in a bowl until well combined. Transfer the mixture to the prepared baking dish and press onto the bottom.
- Pour sweetened condensed milk on graham cracker crust. Sprinkle with an even layer of chocolate chips, coconut, and nuts. Press

toppings down firmly with the back of a fork.
- Bake in the preheated oven until lightly browned, about 25 minutes. Cool completely, then cut into 36 bars or diamonds.

SNOWBALLS

Now these cookies are a family favorite. They usually disappear quickly.

- 1 cup unsalted butter, softened
- ½ cup powdered sugar
- 1 teaspoon vanilla extract
- 2 ¼ cups all-purpose flour
- 1 cup very finely chopped pecans
- ¼ teaspoon salt
- ⅓ cup powdered sugar, or more as needed

Directions

- Gather all ingredients. Preheat the oven to 350 degrees F (175 degrees C).

Beat butter, 1/2 cup powdered sugar, and vanilla with an electric mixer in a large bowl until smooth.

Gradually mix in flour, pecans, and salt until completely incorporated.

Roll dough into walnut-sized balls and place 2 inches apart onto ungreased baking sheets.

Bake in the preheated oven until bottoms are light golden brown but tops are still pale, 12 to 15 minutes. (Try not to let cookies get too brown: it's better to undercook them than to overcook them.)

Remove cookies from the oven and let sit on the baking sheets briefly before removing to wire racks.

Place 1/3 cup powdered sugar in a shallow bowl; roll hot cookies in sugar to coat, then return to the wire racks to cool.

Once cooled, roll cookies in the powdered sugar once more. Just an added note from experience, these cookies can be fragile and tend to break if you try to roll them when they are too hot. They also don't coat properly if they are too cold. I guess, you need to be like Goldilocks and try to get them when the temperature is just right.

About the Author

M. R. Dollschnieder has over a decade in real estate and nearly 20 years writing for local newspapers. She lives in the California desert with her husband, three dogs, four cats and five chickens, spending her days in front of the computer writing and fending off the cat's attempts to assist her by sitting on the keyboard and standing in front of the monitors.

You can connect with me on:

🌐 https://mrdollschniederauthor.com
🐦 https://x.com/MRDollschnieder
📘 https://www.facebook.com/M.R.Dollschnieder.Author
🔗 https://www.tiktok.com/@mr_dollschnieder

Subscribe to my newsletter:

✉ https://mrdollschniederauthor.com/subscribe

Also by M.R. Dollschnieder

Bones in the Backyard
What do hungry pigs have to do with a missing ex? That's the question Holly doesn't want to have to answer.

Bad things have a way of happening to Holly lately and she can't figure out why. A sudden death brings up memories from the past she doesn't want to face. The truth has a way of coming out and this time the consequences could be deadly.

Will she be able to find out who killed her client's husband before there's another victim? What secrets are her fellow agents hiding? The truth is buried somewhere in her past and she's running out of time to find it.

You'll love this intriguing tale with twists and turns and a dose of humor.

Fear at the Fall Festival

What does a bear, a haunted house and a group of elderly women all have in common?

That would be Holly, our local real estate agent with a heart of gold and a knack for attracting the weird and quirky.

Our heroine is fresh off the success of solving two murders and landing the real estate listing of her dreams. Her life appears to finally be settling down and she is looking forward to spending time with her granddaughter and NOT solving a murder because, as she says, she is not a sleuth. Circumstances will once again prove otherwise.

When the chairman of the Fall Festival is no longer available, Holly is thrust into the position. To her dismay, this year it will be held at the Blume House, reputed to be haunted. *Will Holly find love or will murder get in the way?*

Body at the Beach
An open house. A dead body. A missing heir.

A phone call takes Holly and the girls away from their frigid mountain home to the sun and sandy shores of a friend's beach house. A weekend of laying on the sand and watching seagulls fly by sounds idyllic.

Its only natural that they would check out some open houses while in town. Unfortunately, they step through the door into a murder mystery and a missing heir. Can Holly find out who the dead body is? What happened to the baby that was adopted 20 years ago?

Will Holly find her way through the ocean of clues or will she ending up swimming with the fishes?